Torch

The *Devil Souls* Motorcycle Club

LeAnn Ashers

LeAnn Ashers

Copyright © 2016 LeAnn Ashers

All rights reserved

Published by LeAnn Ashers

Designed by: Regina Wamba

Photographer: Wander Aguliar

Formatted by: Brenda Wright, Formatting Done Wright

Torch is a work of fiction. Names, characters, places, and incidents are all products of the author's imagination and are used fictitiously. Any resemblance to actual events, locals, or persons, living or dead, is entirely coincidental.

Except as permitted under the US Copyright Act of 1976, no part of this publication may be reproduced, distributed or transmitted in any form by any means, or stored in a database or retrieval system, without the prior written permission of the author.

dedication

To the girls who thought they would be forever alone because of their disabilities. This is for you. <3

LeAnn Ashers

one

Kayla

I place my hand on the wall, trying to feel my way, as I walk outside in front of the clothing store, where the cab dropped me off. The taxi driver left before I could grab my cane out of his car. A great start to an already fucked-up day. If you haven't figured it out yet, I'm blind. I was born that way; well, at least I think so. You would think I would be used to walking around without being able to see, but I am still terrified to this day.

Where the fuck is the entrance to the store? I swear I should have reached it before now. I asked the taxi driver to drop me off right in front of the door. Of course, he is probably a dick and dropped me off somewhere else.

My hands are starting to get scratched up as I drag them along the brick wall. When I hear a couple of men laugh, I stop and gulp. I close my eyes and will myself to relax, but my heart already feels like it's pounding out of my chest.

Letting out a deep breath, I raise my face and continue forward. I walk along a few more feet until the men's laughter abruptly stops. I stop and wait. I can feel their gazes on me; it feels like my skin is crawling. I shudder and tighten my grip on the wall.

"Need some help?" a man asks. I can hear laughter mixed in with his voice. My heart drops to my feet.

"No, I'm okay," I tell him and try to keep my voice steady. I start taking tiny steps back in the direction I came from, my hands dragging along the wall leaving little cuts on my skin.

"Let me help!" the man insists, and then I feel his hand on my forearm. He pulls me harder than necessary to my right, which I know leads toward the parking lot. Vehicles have been passing me on that side.

Rooting my feet into the concrete, I try to stop him from pulling me. "Let me go." I pull my arms, but his grip tightens on me. I know if I manage to get kidnapped, no one will report me missing.

"Stop!" I say again, but this time I yell, hoping to get my point across. I feel a panic attack looming inside of me. He pulls me harder until I stumble. I raise my fist and swing out in front of me in the hopes of hitting something. More hands grab at my hips and waist. Then I'm airborne as I'm lifted off the ground completely.

I scream at the top of my lungs and buck my body, trying to get them to drop me. I wish I could see, see anything, so I could fight back harder. I hear a man yelling and I scream louder, hoping it helps.

"HELP!"

A hand slaps my mouth before clamping over it. I gag at the smell of the sweat.

All of a sudden, the man holding my shoulders jerks to the side and my head and upper body move toward the ground. Then arms wrap around my waist and I'm pulled away from the men trying to kidnap me.

I'm set on the ground and hear a fist connecting with flesh in front of me. Fist after fist connects with flesh, causing my breathing to get out of control. I'm desperate for air. My hands claw at my neck.

Silence.

That's all I hear in front of me when the sound of fists hitting flesh stops. I hold my breath waiting for what happens next.

When hands touch my face, I flinch away instinctually. "You okay?" my rescuer asks. His voice glides over me like butter and warms me down to my toes. His smell is woodsy and intoxicating.

I'm unable to help myself, I lean forward until my head hits his chest. He wraps his arms around me and tucks me tighter against him. His arms are huge and so warm. Most people would think I am crazy for taking comfort in a stranger like this. But do I give a flying fuck? No.

I hear a thunder of motorcycles and hold tighter to the man in front of me. "You okay, darlin'?" he asks again.

"Yeah, I'm just a bit rattled." I choke out a laugh but can hear the sob in it.

The ground rumbles as the motorcycles pull up beside us. He stands and takes me with him. My head is still on his chest, but my legs are dangling off the ground. "You can put me down." I smile up toward his face; or I hope it's his face.

He sets me on the ground. I rub my hand over my face in disbelief. "I better call the police." I reach into my back pocket, but a hand stops me from taking my phone out.

"No need," he says gruffly when I hear footsteps walking toward us. "What happened, Torch?"

Torch? What kind of name is that? "I was coming out of the store across the road when I saw these three fuckers carrying this woman against her will. They were about to put her in their vehicle in broad fuckin' daylight." Torch grounds out each word, his body vibrating with his anger. "Look at his face, Pres."

"The fuck?" the dude I am assuming is Pres yells. I flinch at his tone. Torch tightens his hand on my waist. He must have felt me flinch.

"Come on, love, let's get you out of here," Torch tells me and nudges me to turn around. I stumble as I trip over a speed bump and flush in embarrassment. "I can't see," I whisper to him.

"Fuck… I'm sorry, darlin'." The next thing I know, I'm lifted off the ground and am carried bridal style, which pisses me off. I may be blind, but I can walk.

"I can walk!"

I feel his body rumble as he chuckles. "I know, but I want to carry you."

Shrugging my shoulders, I decide to enjoy the ride. Who wouldn't? Plus, he rescued me. For a brief moment, I actually thought kidnapped and killed would be how my life would end.

He stops a moment later, and I feel the arm from behind my back shift as the truck presses against me, then hear the click of the door opening a second later. He lifts me higher until I feel the leather of the seat against my butt. I move my arm from behind his neck and into my lap.

The truck door slams. It's hot in here from the air being turned off for a while. But the truck still has that new car smell. I can tell it's a truck by the amount of room and how high he had to lift me into the seat.

The driver's side door opens, and I smell and hear Torch get inside. The door slams shut, then the truck roars to life with the air conditioner on full blast. I feel us moving.

"Where are we going?" I ask, because I realize I didn't give him my address.

"To my house," he says nonchalantly. *Umm, what?*

"Umm, what?" I voice my thoughts.

"To my house," he repeats as I feel the truck speed up. My heart starts to beat out of my chest. "Put your seatbelt on."

"I want to go home," I whisper and feel the tears threatening to break through. I feel so out of control and don't know where I'm going. I have a feeling he won't hurt me, but...

His phone rings, and he answers it. I chew on my bottom lip nervously. "Hey, baby girl."

Pause.

Then, "All right, be careful. Take your taser and pepper spray. Love you. Bye." He hangs up and tells me, "That was my daughter, Paisley."

Grabbing my hair tie off my wrist, I tie my hair up on top of my head in a messy bun. "How old is your daughter?"

"She just turned nineteen and is away at college. I had her when I was eighteen years old and raised her myself." I can hear how proud he is of her.

"Wow." He raised her by himself when he was eighteen years old? What guy can say that for himself? Not many, that's for sure.

"You got any kids?" Torch asks me.

I shake my head no. "No."

"You have a man?" he asks next. I hear the steering wheel crunch as if he is fisting it very hard.

"No, I'm single," I say hesitantly, wondering why he is acting angry all of a sudden.

"Good," I hear him mutter under his breath. *Umm, what?* Yeah, I'm not touching that.

Then I remember I need to send some files to my formatter tonight. "I need to go home. I have to work."

"What do you do?'

I know what he is going to say when I tell him I'm an author, so I'll answer that for him. "I'm a romance author. I have a special computer and headset. I talk into the headset and it does what I want, including typing and so on."

"We can swing by your house and get your laptop."

"Okay," I agree, but I'm not going to his house. I want to send the doc and sleep the rest of the day away to forget about this horrible day.

two

Kayla

"Torch!" I scream and pound his back with the sides of my fists as he carries me out of my apartment. Once he realized I was planning on staying, he lifted me over his shoulder and carried me right back out of the apartment.

"Let me down. This is kidnapping!" I smack his back and squirm, trying to get down.

Whack!

I stop squirming. I can't believe he just did that. He just smacked my butt, and hard at that. "I can't believe you just did that," I say in disbelief.

He chuckles and playfully smacks my butt again. "Believe it, baby."

He deposits me back in the truck, sets my laptop in my lap, and slams the door shut. Of course, I open my door, but before I do, I wait a second or two for him to get to the driver's side.

I place my laptop under my arm and hop out. I land on my feet, but my ankles yell at me in pain from the long drop. Still, I run forward, hoping my apartment is in that direction. I barely make it two feet when I'm picked up again.

"Oh my God! I'm going to murder you!" I hiss at him and whack him in the head with my laptop. He laughs at me then sets me in the truck again, but this time he grabs hold of my hand and has me scoot over so I can't make a break for it. *Damn you, Torch.* I am going to catch him asleep and make him pay.

Torch starts his truck and then we are off to God knows where. I cross my arms over my chest and pout. Torch laughs at me, and a finger touches my bottom lip where it sticks out. I gasp and pull away, not having expected him to do that. I uncross my arms. His hand grabs mine and lifts it off my lap, then his lips touch the back of my hand; they are full and warm. I shudder at the touch.

I usually get to know someone by touching them. Their face, arms, hands. When I touch them, I can feel their body movements. Of course, I can hear things, too. Like someone entering a room, something being moved, or when someone is moving on the couch getting comfortable. I always count my steps from one end of the room to the other and make sure everything is in the same place; and if things are accidentally moved and are in the wrong spot, I fall, and it's not gracefully at all.

Sighing, I give in to him, knowing that if I fight any more, it will be futile. "Why won't you let me go home?"

He places our joined hands into his lap. I try to hide my reaction to that. "It's not safe."

My heart stops, "What do you mean?" My voice trembles slightly. *Those men aren't going to come back, are they? They can't know where I live*, I think to myself in panic.

Torch shifts in his seat, "Those men are part of a gang, a gang that's a part of a trafficking ring. They have been out of the city for almost three years and still are. They could just be passing through. Still, to be safe, you need to stay with me. I will protect you."

Sydney told me all about her story about gang members and her being kidnapped. Could it be connected? She told me they had gang symbols on their faces.

"Do they have gang symbols on their faces?" I ask Torch, hoping I am wrong.

I feel his body stiffen and fear the worst. "Yeah. How did you know that?" he asks. I can feel him looking at me again, which makes me more nervous.

"My friend, Sydney, was kidnapped by a gang and the members had gang symbols on their faces."

"Kane's woman?"

"Yep," I mutter and rest my head on the back of the seat. Which is the middle of the seat. I still haven't scooted over. The toll of the day is finally catching up with me.

"Relax, darlin'," Torch whispers and kisses the top of my head, surprising me all over again. I don't get this guy at all. I just met him, but my stomach flutters with butterflies. I haven't felt that since I was a teenager, which was when my crush kissed me for the first time.

We sit in silence until we reach his house. When the truck stops, I hear what sounds like a gate opening before he starts driving again. The gate bangs shut a few seconds later. "We're here," he tells me. I sit up pulling my laptop into my lap. I feel Torch get out of the vehicle beside me and turn in his direction. His hand takes mine to help me toward the door.

I run my fingers along the back of the seat as I push myself closer to Torch. He grabs my hips, then lifts me out of the truck. I stumble a bit as I step on loose gravel, but my hand is fastened tightly in Torch's as he slams the truck door closed.

I need a service dog. It would make my life a lot easier, but I could never afford one. I feel like I should be scared right now, because I don't know this person. But I think if he was going to hurt me, he would have done so before now, and he sure wouldn't have rescued me from those guys.

For the first time in my life, I am deciding to trust a stranger, and blindly at that. I am taking a leap of faith, and that's something I never ever do. I fear the unknown.

"Steps in front of you," Torch warns me.

We walk up the front steps and then stop. I hear keys jingling as he unlocks the door then the door creaks as it opens. Torch leads me inside the house. The cold of the house hits me in the face and raises goose bumps on my arms.

"Let's order pizza and relax, what do you say?" Torch asks me as I sit down on the couch once I feel it touch the back of my legs.

Smiling, I say, "Sure."

He makes the call before he plops down onto the couch directly beside me.

Torch

Kayla fell asleep after we ate the pizza and she listened to the TV. She's lying on her side with her head on my leg, her curly hair fanned behind her. She's the most beautiful woman I have ever seen. Her eyes are the darkest green I have ever encountered. I could stare at them all day.

I gently lift her head from my lap and transfer it onto a pillow. Bending down, I lift her up in my arms, hugging her to my chest. She moans and moves deeper into my body, startling me. Unable to resist, I bend my head down and sniff her hair, breathing in her scent. Heaven. That's what she smells like.

She threw me a fucking curveball when she said she was blind, which made my protective instincts kick into overdrive. Watching her almost get kidnapped will forever be branded in my brain, as will feeling the fear pouring off of her.

Walking to *my* bedroom, I lay her in the middle of the bed then grab the waistband of her leggings and start to pull them down her legs. Her hands smack me, and her eyes fly open.

She grabs at her chest and stares into nothing. I can tell I scared her. Fuck. "Shhh, baby, I was undressing you for bed. You fell asleep." I place my hand on her arm so she knows where I am. She relaxes and settles into the bed.

"You have something I can change into?" her meek voice asks as she runs her hands up and down her legs nervously.

I get off the bed and walk over to the dresser, where I grab one of my shirts for her to sleep in. "Raise your arms over your head. I will help you."

"I can do it." Her voice trembles. Not wanting her to be even more scared, I give in.

"Here." I set the shirt in her lap and watch as she feels inside of it and tries to find the tag in the back before she lifts her shirt over her head, leaving her in a bra that barely keeps her tits at bay. My already semi-hard dick is now hard enough to pound nails.

Now isn't the time for that shit considering the day she fucking had, but my dick has a mind of its own.

She slips my tee over her head and then reaches down to her leggings and pulls them down, dropping them onto the floor.

Does she know I am still here? No way in hell am I going to tell her. I am not a gentleman. Smiling to myself, I watch as she reaches under her shirt and then pulls her bra off. Damn. My eyes zero in on her freed breasts, her nipples peeking through the fabric.

Fuck me. This is torture.

"Where is the bathroom?" she asks, and my head shoots up from her tits to her face. I can see a small smile on her face. The little shit knew I was watching the whole time.

"It's straight across the room. Want me to show you?"

She nods, so I grab her hand to help her off the bed. She is counting the steps to the bathroom under her breath. I lead her inside and place her hand on the sink, toilet, even the shower so she knows where everything is.

She grabs my forearm and glides her hand down so she is holding my hand, and smiles, "I want to thank you for everything. Seriously, most people wouldn't have been this generous."

I don't answer her. Instead, I glide my hand up her arm to her neck until I'm clutching her face. I place my lips on her forehead. *What is wrong with me? I never act like this.* I back out of the room, pulling the door closed behind me, and walk over to the bed and slip out of my pants, leaving me only in my boxers.

Pulling back the blankets on the bed, I climb in. I lie back onto the pillows with my arms behind my head. The door creaks slightly as she walks out of the bathroom. Her mouth moves as she counts. When she reaches the bed, she climbs on and crawls up toward me.

I touch her arms, causing her to jump slightly. Then I pick her up and set her on the bed beside me. "You're sleeping here, too?" The confusion and nervousness are clear in her voice.

"It's a big bed," I tell her and try not to look at her tits, because her nipples are hard again.

She blushes. I grin. Then she grabs the end of the blanket, sticks her feet under it, and pulls it up under her chin, then up and around her face. She is so wrapped up in the blanket I can only see half of her face.

"You're staring. I feel it," she mumbles and closes her eyes.

"Yeah." I drop down onto my pillows and clap to turn off the bedroom lights. This is the first time I have slept in the same bed with a woman since my daughter's mother was around. She had Paisley, handed her to me, and said she was too young to have a kid; and that was that. She left without looking back. I wasn't taking a chance for her to take my baby girl away from me, so I made sure she signed her rights away.

I raised my baby girl from day one, paid a babysitter when I worked all day. Then I came home and took care of her. Been with her through every sickness, her first steps, all of her scrapes and cuts, at her first day of school. All of her firsts. I also made sure she was raised following the values in life and owning the self-respect so many girls lack nowadays.

Three years ago was when one of my worst nightmares almost became reality, but thankfully, my baby girl was saved before anything could happen. That day changed her life forever, as it did mine. She wasn't my same daughter for a long time. She wasn't as innocent and it broke my heart. Then she started taking kickboxing and self-defense classes and changed before my eyes. She is now even more confident than she was before the attack, because she now knows she is able to defend herself. The bastard who tried to hurt her isn't breathing any longer; but now she is at college surrounded by dickheads. Fuck me.

"What are you thinking about so hard over there?" Kayla interrupts my thoughts.

"My daughter."

"Is something wrong?"

I look over at her. She has her eyes closed, looking incredibly comfortable with her hair splayed out behind her on the pillow.

"No, I miss the little shit," I tell her honestly.

She laughs out loud and grins from ear-to-ear. "I bet she's beautiful."

Thinking about her, I smile. "She really is. Too beautiful. I had to chase too many pretty boys away from her." She used to get so mad, but if a guy liked her enough, he wouldn't have given in so easily. Pussies. All of them pussies.

Kayla laughs again and rubs her eyes. "I bet she loved that."

"She hated it, but I don't give a shit. Those boys aren't good enough for my baby girl," I answer gruffly, thinking about the guys trying to catch her. She's never getting married if I can help it.

"Aww!" Kayla drawls out and turns over, facing me. She reaches out her hands until it hits my chest then moves it up until she touches my cheeks and gives them both a squeeze. "That's so sweet!"

Rolling my eyes, I move her hands from my cheeks, but I don't let go of them. "Get some sleep."

"Night, Torch."

"Good night, sweetheart."

In the middle of the night I sense something is wrong. I lay still and listen for what woke me up. I hear soft crying and click on the bedside lamp. Kayla is clutching her pillow and blanket to her as hard as she can.

"Please, let me go." She sobs and buries her head in the pillow like she is trying to hide from her dreams. I know what happened earlier today is messing with her dreams. It haunts her, and it pisses me the fuck off that something so tragic has happened to her to be affected like this. Nobody should be scared like that.

I touch her back gently, trying to wake her without freaking her the fuck out. "Kayla, shh. You're dreaming. Wake up, baby." I shake her back gently.

Her eyes shoot open and her mouth opens wide as she gasps for air. She runs her hands up and down her body and then covers her face, letting out deep breaths.

"Torch?" she softly calls for me.

I reach out and hug her to me. I can't resist. "Right here." My mouth touches the crown of her head. She sighs and burrows her chest into my shoulder.

I can't resist asking her. "Baby, what were you dreaming?"

Her whole entire body stiffens before it starts to tremble.

I hold her tightly, as if I could stop her from shaking.

"I was dreaming I was kidnapped. That I wasn't rescued. And they were doing horrible things to me." Her head shakes from side to side like she is trying to force the images out of her head. It fucking makes me mad that she has to feel this way. What gives a man the fucking right to take what isn't theirs? The earth should be rid of scum like that, the world would be a better fucking place; and I am just the fucking man to do that.

"I won't make you, baby, but I am here if you need to talk." I rub her back soothingly. She nods, her shoulders shaking. She's crying. I can't deal with tears. They make me feel helpless; and I fucking hate that.

Kayla

I'm crying against Torch's shoulder. He saw me have a nightmare. It's so fucking embarrassing. I'm more than embarrassed. I'm afraid he will look at me differently. Those men terrified me. I knew what was going to happen to me. They belong to a trafficking ring.

I had a shitty life growing up until I moved in with my grandparents when I was eleven years old. My dad loved to torture me because I was blind. He would purposely move things in front of me as I was walking, so I would fall and get hurt. He would throw things and hit me in the face, because I couldn't see them coming. It was pure hell. I walked on eggshells, and to this day I still do. It's engrained in me.

My mother isn't a great mother, she didn't protect me then like a mother should, so I suffered the consequences. She only worried about him. He's all she cares about. He treats her like shit, treated her kid like shit; it seemed like the more he hurt her or me, the more she loved him.

When I stop crying, I fall back asleep against Torch's shoulder, exhausted. I take comfort in this man's arms, which is something I haven't ever allowed myself to do before. I am a thirty-year-old woman and have had one lover in my life, but I kicked him out when we were done having sex. Well, when he was done. I was just a warm body. I have a hard time trusting and letting people in.

three

Kayla

"Wake up, baby," Torch grumbles in his sleepy voice. Cracking my eyes open, all I see is darkness. I wish more than anything I could see, but it's not possible. My optometrist says it's impossible, though I'm afraid he isn't a very good doctor.

"Morning." I rub my eyes and feel what I'm lying on. I'm completely on top of Torch, my legs on either side of him, my face against his bare, naked, muscular chest. I blush and lift myself off of him.

Fingers touch my cheeks, and I bet they turn even redder. I have always been a blusher, or so I've been told, and can feel the burn as they get hotter.

"What do you want for breakfast?" Torch pulls me back down onto his chest and rubs his hands up and down my bare back, because my shirt has ridden up. My panties must be showing, but I can't bring myself to be embarrassed. Who could be embarrassed of something they haven't ever seen?

What a way to wake up, though. I could get used to this.

That's a scary thought.

My life went from boring to out of control in a split second. I'm not sure how to deal. I was almost kidnapped yesterday, and then I was sort of...err...kidnapped by Torch, if you could call it that. He carried me over his shoulder against my will. So I guess it would be called kidnapped.

"It doesn't matter to me," I finally answer him. His hand goes to my butt, then he sits up in bed and slides off, carrying me with him when he stands up. I'm going to actively ignore his morning wood pressing against some place that desperately wants it.

My arms go around his neck when I feel us going down the stairs. "Please, don't drop me!" I hold tighter. If I'm going down, he's going with me.

He chuckles and holds me tighter in his arms. It's more like his hands tightening on my butt. Once we reach the bottom, he walks for a few seconds before he sets me on a counter top. I can tell from the coldness of the surface and my feet dangling off the ground.

I can tell he opens the fridge by the clatter of stuff moving around along with glass jars hitting against each other.

"Let me help. I cook all the time at my house." I scoot to the edge of the bar and stretch my feet down until I touch the ground. But before I can push myself off the counter, Torch grabs my hips and pushes me back.

His hand touches my face. "Let me take care of you," he whispers, and I swear I can feel his breath right at my lips. Gulping, I let out a deep sigh because of how close to my lips he is. "Okay."

He lets go of me and goes back to work. The room is silent besides the noises of him frying bacon and moving throughout the room. Things are scraping the top of the counter, hitting against each other. It's silent, and I start to feel nervous when I don't know what's happening around me.

My life has changed so much in the past day. I feel like I'm getting whiplash. Usually, I'm rolling out of bed and into my kitchen to prepare breakfast myself. I have everything in my kitchen memorized, know all the spices by taste, scent, and feel. If I know my surroundings, I can take care of myself, but this is different altogether. I can't remember the last time someone made me breakfast.

Being blind is exactly how it sounds. You go into every situation completely blind, exposed, and vulnerable. You don't know what's directly in front of you, you can't see if something is coming toward you or is going to hurt you. I have been knocked down by people too many times to count. I have been taunted. I have gone into the wrong stores, because people have given me the wrong directions just to be mean.

I don't want pity, as I'm not helpless. If there's a will, there's a way. But every blind person knows the fear I'm talking about. I don't have family to help me, but I do what I need to do. I have made it for twelve years by myself and will continue to do so.

I must admit being taken care of like this feels nice. Beyond nice, though it isn't expected. Torch continues to shock me. I'm not used to this. When I lived at home with my parents, I lived off of meals that came from a box or a bag. My grandmother attempted to cook for me, but she was old, so cooking didn't come easy to her.

"It's ready," Torch interrupts my thoughts, and I move my head in the direction of his voice.

I step down off the counter, and his hand touches my forearm to lead me to the dining room table. The seat makes a noise as he pulls it out for me. "The chair is directly beside you." Smiling to myself, I duck my head before he can see. I sit down and touch the edge of the table.

I hear him walk out of the room and then back in. He sets a plate in front of me as well as something else. "Your fork's on the right side of your plate, and your milk is in front of that."

His chair scoots out beside me, and I hear it creak as he sits down. I lift my hand in front of me and to the right. It touches my pancake and the syrup gets on my fingers.

Torch grabs my hand, and I think he's going to lead me to my fork. But instead, he sticks my fingers into his mouth to get rid of the syrup. I gasp at the feel of his mouth on my skin. I can't believe he did that. "I can't believe you did that," I voice my thoughts.

"Believe it." He chuckles and sets my hand on my fork.

I shake my head in disbelief then cut up my pancake and run my fork over the pieces to gauge how large they are before I stab a piece and take a bite. Mmmm, homemade. He can cook, too? How is he still single?

"I'll do the dishes. Just show me where they are." I suggest once I finish my food.

"No, I'll do them." He starts to take my plate away, but I grip the sides so he isn't able to.

"No, I'll do it," I tell him more sternly and stand up.

I turn in the direction of the kitchen, because I know that much. Torch grunts, and I can actually hear him grinding his teeth. Hmm. He must not like being told no. I shall do that more often.

"No," he growls again and tries to lead me back to my seat.

"Torch, I swear to goodness, let me do the fucking dishes!" I say to him, louder.

Then he starts laughing, and I almost do, too, because it's contagious. "Damn, baby, you have some claws." I can almost imagine his smirk. He seems like a guy who smirks.

"You bet." I wink. "Now, show me the sink."

During the next few minutes, I wash the dishes while he puts them away.

I set the dishcloth on the counter once I'm done. Torch's hands grip my own and he turns me around so I'm facing him. His arm bands around my waist, and he sets my hand on his shoulder. Then his other hand holds my right hand in his. A song comes over the radio. *From the Ground Up* by Dan + Shay.

My heart stops in my chest as he starts to sway from side to side with me in his arms.

Who is this person? I just met him, so why is he holding me like this? What does dancing to a song like this mean?

Torch presses his lips to my forehead, and I close my eyes when I almost start crying. This moment is so emotional. I don't get it.

As the song continues, he sways with me from side to side. I lay my head on his chest, feeling content; it's a strange feeling. "I know this sounds crazy to you, baby, but I want to see where this leads. I want you to be mine," Torch murmurs against the top of my head. My heart stops at his words, yet I know I want this. If he is half as good to me as he is now, I want nothing more. I want it all. All he will give me and I will give him all of me.

I raise my head toward his and smile. "I want nothing more."

It's time for me to take a leap of faith for once and face the unknown. It's a scary thing facing the mysterious, but it's time for me to live. I realized yesterday how quickly your life could be taken away.

"Good, 'cause I won't take no for an answer." He chuckles and pinches my butt. I laugh and smack his chest. Grinning, I tuck a stray hair behind my ear. Torch tightens his hand on mine and leads me out of the kitchen. I count my steps as I walk along.

When my knees touch the couch, I turn around and sit down. I feel Torch sit down beside me. One of his arms goes under my legs and the other behind my back, lifting me up into his lap. I sigh and tuck my head in the crook of his neck, where I breathe in his woodsy scent. It's intoxicating.

He trails his fingers up and down my back. Closing my eyes, I relax my whole entire body, enjoying his touch.

"Do you need to call someone?" Torch asks but doesn't stop his movements on my back.

"There's no one to call," I tell him softly and realize that nobody truly cares about me enough to know if I am dead or alive. It's sad when you think about it. I've never had someone I could count on, especially not since my grandparents died. I am utterly alone in the world.

"No one?" I can hear the disbelief in his voice.

I shake my head against his shoulder.

"I thought I heard you mention you had a mom?" He smoothes my hair over my shoulder, his hand trailing against my neck. Being blind, touch means everything.

When someone is touching you, you at least know a bit of what's happening. Touch lets me see by feeling.

"I do, but we aren't close," I tell him simply, hoping he will change the subject.

"Why?"

Shit, I think to myself.

I guess my hope is thwarted. "She's not the best mom, and I am better off without her. She lives two hours away." My parents live in a trailer, a trailer that is rat infested. I've repeatedly asked her to leave and come stay with me. But she still stays with him. I don't get her infatuation. He is mean to her every single day, hits her, and made my life hell. She thinks once you are married, you shouldn't leave, no matter what. It's a wife's duty to serve her husband. *Puhlease*. I would rather be alone for the rest of my life than be with someone who is remotely similar to my father.

Torch stiffens for a second before he lets out a deep breath. "I know there is more to the story. But I won't pressure you to tell me. For now."

I heard the *for now* loud and clear.

four

Kayla

Torch carries me up the stairs for bed. We've spent the whole day eating, cuddling on the couch, and just relaxing. Today was one of the best days of my life. I haven't ever felt this completely at ease before. Safety and security oozes off of him.

I laugh at Torch as I feel him fondling my butt cheeks and reach back to smack his hand. "Watch your hands there, big boy."

Another thing I have noticed with Torch is he is handsy but not in a creepy way. It's just the way he is. I have to admit he has my body on edge from the 'innocent' little touches that have happened throughout the day. I'm enjoying it. I already brushed my teeth thirty or so minutes ago. I wanted to grab my phone from downstairs, but of course Torch just had to carry me.

Torch lets go of me, and I scream for a second before I land on top of the bed. "You dick!" I hold my chest. I thought he had fallen with me or dropped me.

He laughs, and I feel the bed move as he climbs in with me. I pout and cross my arms over my chest. I feel Torch crawling closer to me, but I don't move.

His lips touch mine. I gasp, because I wasn't expecting that. When I do, my mouth opens and he takes the advantage to deepen the kiss. I lift my hands to his face and tilt my head so I can deepen the kiss even more. Torch's tongue runs over the seam of my lips before his teeth capture my bottom lip. He bites down gently, and I press my lips harder against his.

He pulls away and chuckles huskily. "Think twice about pouting again, won't you?"

He set my body on fire with that kiss and thinks it's over just like that? Nah, when I said I was diving into this headfirst, I meant it.

My hand is still on his face. I move it to the back of his head then pull his face toward me and press my lips hard back against his. He growls and sticks his hand into my hair, pulling slightly so he can take control of the kiss.

Then I am laid back onto the bed with him between my legs. The heat of him on me there has me groaning, and I can't resist rubbing myself against his belly. Torch slowly slides his hand down my stomach, then to my waist and inside of my panties. My eyes shoot open at the feel of his hand so close to my…

"Let me take care of you," he whispers, his breath touching my kiss-swollen lips. I shudder and let out a deep sigh. I feel anxious waiting for his next move. He takes my mouth with his again, caressing as if he was making love to it. *Who am I to argue?*

Lifting my hips, I help him take off my panties. His hand touches my clit, and my body twitches. I have always been super sensitive.

I moan against his lips when his middle and forefinger enter me. My hands tighten in his hair. Those two fingers cause a pinch of pain for a split second, because it's been a while.

He leisurely moves them inside me while his thumb moves against my clit. My toes start to curl as the orgasm pulls close. It's so close I can almost reach it. Then he curls his fingers and hits that spot. My legs tremble and I scream as the most powerful orgasm I've ever had flows through me. I hold on to him as I come down from the high. He pulls his fingers from me, and then I hear him sucking on something.

Oh God. Did he?

I feel my face flame with embarrassment. Oh my God.

"Are you embarrassed?" he asks much to my horror.

"You...umm." I wave my hand in the air, hoping he gets it and I won't have to explain.

He chuckles, and I get even hotter. I'm pretty sure I am blushing to my toes now. "I couldn't resist getting a taste of your pussy."

Ground, swallow me up.

"Oh my God," I whisper to myself over and over.

"Haven't you ever had a man go down on you?" I can hear the amusement in his voice. He's reveling in my embarrassment. I hide my face with my hand, as my face gets even hotter. "No," I whisper, hoping he won't hear me and lets it go.

"What was that?" he whispers in my face, and I jump.

I sigh and lift my hands from my face. "No."

He growls, and I feel his hand on my pussy again, holding it like he is claiming it. "What kind of fucking men have you been with? Though, I'm glad I will be your first."

I don't know what to say to that, so I don't say anything. I feel Torch lie down on the bed. Then he pulls me over so I am lying on top of his chest. "Good night, sweetheart."

"Good night, Torch."

Groaning, I stretch my hands above my head. When a hand moves on my waist, I can't keep the smile off my face. My life has done a complete one-eighty in just a few days, but one thing I know is that I wouldn't change a thing.

"Good morning, baby," Torch whispers against the side of my neck, his breath raising goose bumps on my skin.

"Morning." I reach over and touch his head, running my fingers through his hair. He lets out a sigh and burrows deeper into the side of my neck. Using my fingernails, I scratch the top of his head and giggle when he sighs again along with smacking his mouth together like a little kid.

I feel his head lifting off my shoulder and can feel him staring at me. "You laughing at me, baby?"

I suck my lips into my mouth and shake my head no. His lips touch the skin under my jaw, and I let my lips open at the feel of his. "I believe you're lying to me."

Raising my hand, I pinch my thumb and forefinger together. "Just a little bit."

"Thought so," he grumbles. His hand slides down my body, stopping at the top of my pussy. I hold my breath waiting for his next move. When he taps my clit, I jump and hiss through my teeth.

He chuckles while his lips keep touching my cheek. I can't help but smile. "I think you need to be punished."

That takes the smile off my face instantly. I gulp, loudly. "Wh-what do you mean?" I stutter and touch his shoulder.

"Hands above your head," he growls. I bite my lip, but do as I'm told. The sheet is ripped off me, leaving me completely naked. I feel beyond exposed. I can't see what's happening and feel too open, so I move my hands toward my breasts.

He stops my movements and raises them back above my head. "Don't hide yourself from me. I would never hurt you in any way. I haven't seen anyone as beautiful as you. The only kind of punishment you'll get from me is a raw throat from screaming my name as I make you come"—he stops and licks my nipple—"over"—he stops again and sucks my hard nipple deep into his mouth—"and over"—his mouth trails down to my belly button, leaving kisses in his wake—"again," he says last and latches onto my clit. I scream at the sudden intense feeling.

"Oh my God," I chant over and over at the feel of his tongue lapping. When it enters me, I scream again, because this feeling is so erotic it's almost too much.

His tongue goes back to my clit, as his finger enters my pussy. I throw my head back. When he adds another finger, my legs start trembling. He growls, and my eyes roll into the back of my head.

I can't help but scream while I experience the most powerful orgasm of my life. My whole body shakes and moves uncontrollably as shock wave after shock wave hits me. Torch's body covers mine, his arms wrapping around me

My head falls to the side as my soul returns to my body. I can't move and am not sure I will ever be the same again.

"You okay?" Torch chuckles cockily, and I don't move or say a word. I close my eyes. My body is still shaking. Torch smoothes the hair out of my face, and I smile slightly at his sweetness.

"I'm not sure I'll ever be the same." I run my hand over my face.

"More where that came from."

I can imagine him smirking right now. Shaking my head, I lift my hand until I touch his face then follow with my head. My lips hit his nose, so I drift down to his lips to give him a sweet, short kiss.

I pull away and lie back down onto the bed. Torch rolls over and takes me with him, so I'm now lying on top of his chest. Closing my eyes, I attempt to go back to sleep when the doorbell rings.

"I'll be back, babe. It's just one of my brothers." He kisses the top of my head before he scoots out of bed. I fall onto a pillow and wrap my arm around it, clutching it to me.

I kind of want to follow him and see who's down there. I remember how many steps it takes to get downstairs and into the living room. Sitting up, I scoot off the bed on my butt until my feet touch the ground.

There's a shirt under my feet, so I use my toes to pick it up. Pulling it over my head, I move my foot around some more until I find a pair of my sleep shorts. Using my toes again, I lift them up to me then put them on.

I reach over and touch the lamp beside the bed to get an idea where I am. I count my steps until I reach the door, then walk out into the hallway until I reach the wall opposite of me. I count my steps again until I reach the stairway. My hand holds on to the rail, and I walk down them with ease.

Halfway down, I hear a few men talking. The only voice I recognize is Torch's. When I hit the living room floor, the talking halts.

"Who is this?" a deep voice asks.

"None of your fucking business. And stop staring at her like that," Torch yells at the man. I can hear the anger in his voice. I can't help but secretly love every bit of his alphaness.

"Why won't you look at me?" the same voice asks, and my head shoots up, ashamed. I stare into nothing as my face flames with embarrassment, but then I raise my chin up. I won't let that comment get me down.

"I'm blind," I state and cross my arms over my chest. Then I walk farther into the living room, counting my steps under my breath as I go along. Torch throws his arms around me and tucks me into his side.

Torch

I don't hear her walk down the stairs while I am talking to Techy until she gets to the bottom and that damn step creaks. I look over and she is literally every fucking man's wet dream wearing my shirt and her hair mussed up slightly. Her face has that freshly fucked look.

Damn, she's fucking hot.

I remember my MC brothers and see them staring at her. Staring at *my* Kayla. My temper flares, and I want to rip their fucking eyeballs out of their heads and erase her from their minds. Nobody sees her underdressed like this but me. She's wearing my shirt and a pair of shorts that are barely visible below the bottom of the shirt.

"None of your fucking business. And stop staring at her like that," I yell at Techy and our enforcer, Ryan, who came out to discuss the gang members being in town. We got rid of those fuckers two years ago.

Techy smiles that shit-eating grin of his, while Ryan raises an eyebrow. I let out a deep breath and pinch the bridge of my nose. I don't give two flying fucks what they think.

"Why won't you look at me?" Techy asks Kayla. Is that fucker that fucking stupid, or does he have a death wish? Ryan stares at Techy like he is the dumbest fucker in the world.

I take a step toward him, ready to pummel the inconsiderate prick.

"I'm blind," Kayla tells him with her head raised high. I can't help but feel proud of her right now. Someone says something so fucking stupid, yet she brushes it off.

She starts walking across the room, and I meet her halfway, tucking her under my arm.

"I'm sorry," Techy apologizes, and I see her smile. She's too fucking sweet, which doesn't help me not feel protective of her. I want to protect that sweetness and keep her pure.

If I were a good guy, I would stay away and not taint her. I have killed, tortured, and done a lot of fucked-up things. I didn't get the name Torch from nowhere. But I have only killed and tortured in the name of my club and protecting my family. Never without reason. And people will be able to sleep easy without those fuckers on the street.

"It's okay," Kayla's angel voice accepts, as she smiles fully now, showing those dimples. I watch Techy and see him get that sheened look in his eyes. Hell. No.

Ryan sees it and smacks him on the back of the head. I nod my thanks to him. Techy is a goofy fucker, but he's amazing with computers, saved all of our asses a couple times.

"We are going to the diner to eat breakfast," Vin says. It's an invitation.

"Wanna go, baby?" She nods then moves out of my arms, and I see her counting under her breath until she walks up the stairs completely at ease.

As soon as she is up the stairs and out of view, Techy looks at me with his mouth agape.

"Damn. Did you see the ass and tits on that girl?" He whistles, and I snap. I punch him in the face as hard as I can. He stumbles back a few steps.

"You are one dumb fucker." Vin laughs and shakes his head.

Techy just smiles that goofy smile. "She is, though." He walks to the other side of the room, away from me. Smart. I grab my cut off the back of the couch and slip it on. I got dressed before coming down the stairs. One perk of being a man; we only have to grab a clean pair of jeans and a black shirt.

A few minutes later, she comes back down the stairs wearing skinny jeans and a tight V-neck shirt. God help me. Why the fuck must they make clothes like that? Techy's mouth falls open. I smack it closed before I walk over to Kayla.

Kayla

We fly down the highway on Torch's motorcycle. It's the most amazing feeling. I'm wrapped around his back. Even though I can't see a thing, it's so freeing feeling the wind and sun on my face while I can hear his three MC buddies roar down the highway beside us.

A few minutes later, we slow down and stop only seconds after. Torch climbs off and grips my waist to lift me off the bike. I take my helmet and leather jacket off, which I am assuming are his daughter's.

He takes my hand and leads me. It would have been easier if I had my walking stick so I could walk myself without assistance, but I am sure even if I weren't blind, he would behave the same way.

"A step in front of you," he tells me, and I step up.

I hear the diner door open and touch the side of it as we walk inside. By the sounds of it, Torch's three friends enter behind us.

"Scoot in the booth," Torch orders. I reach forward to touch the table, then reach down and touch the booth seat before I bend to sit in the seat and scoot over. I feel Torch sit down beside me. Then there's a sound of a chair getting pulled over. I am assuming it's for one of the guys, because I don't think all three will want to sit in a seat together.

A menu touches my hand, so I wrap my hand around it. "Want me to read it to you?" Torch asks, and I smile with relief.

He reads me the entire menu. The waitress comes over five times during that time, interrupting him. I can hear the sneer in her voice as she asks if he is finished yet. *Rude much?* Why must girls be bitches all the freaking time?

On the sixth time she pops over, we are finally ready to order. I decided to just get a hamburger, but have already forgotten what they call it. I know it sounded delicious with melted blue cheese and all of the works.

Torch orders for me, but stops halfway through and falls completely silent. Feeling uneasy, I grab his arm.

"What's your problem?" Torch growls.

"Is she retarded or something? Can't she order herself, or is she too stupid to read?" the bitch waitress sneers. I can feel the heat of her gaze on me.

Oh. No. She. Didn't.

Did I mention I have a temper?

"Bitch, you better not be talking about me," I warn her oh so calmly.

"Who else would I be I talking about?" she cackles, then something hits me in the face. I jerk and catch what she hit me with.

I sit calmly for a second and take ahold of my drink. "Duck," I tell Torch and his buddies then stand up in my seat, lean forward quickly, and grab the bitch's shirt. She squeals and scratches at my hand, trying to pull it loose, but I splash my drink directly in her face and then push her chest. Pieces of ice are still in the cup, so I reach inside and grab a handful before I lift her shirt open and drop them inside, then I let go of it and pat her chest hard.

"Oh shit!" Techy laughs.

I sit back down in my seat and grab the napkin she threw at me to wipe my hands. "Now, go get my food and a new drink, bitch." I wave my hand, dismissing her.

"Damn, Kayla!" Torch laughs in disbelief. I shrug. I may be fucking blind, but I'm not a pushover.

"No, she isn't going back to work. You're fired, bitch," Torch growls at her when I feel him stand up. "You have ten fucking seconds to get out of this restaurant. The Devil's Souls MC owns this place."

I can hear her shoes slapping the ground as she runs away and can't keep the grin off my face. Serves her right.

"I'll get Jackie to fix our food," Ryan says, and I hear the booth creak as he stands.

"Kayla, you're like the sweetest little shit, but then you got pissed and I saw the devil pop out," Techy says and starts laughing.

I grin from ear-to-ear, glad they approve of my crazy. Torch laughs right along with him. I lay my head on his shoulder, feeling happy.

A few minutes later, I hear plates being set on the table, the glass clacking against the top. My hand is lying on the table, and I feel the plate hit it. Reaching onto my plate, I touch my burger and fries to get a feel of where everything is.

I grab a napkin, set it in my lap, and take my burger with both hands, raising it toward my mouth and taking a huge bite. We eat in silence with Torch touching my leg one too many times for it to be an accident.

Once Torch and the guys pay, Torch rests his hand on the small of my back as we walk out of the diner. I feel completely safe with him. I just can't explain it. I've dated plenty of times, but none of those guys touch the scale of how Torch is with me. I've been left on a date in a restaurant because the guy was embarrassed by being seen with me.

"What was the waitress' deal?" I ask him as we walk toward his motorcycle.

He sighs and moves his arm so I am tucked against his side. "She is a hang-around wanting to be an ole lady."

"Ahhh," I draw out and shake my head. "Bitches be crazy." I laugh at the thought of that stupid waitress. She totally made a fool of herself. Maybe she'll think twice about being a bitch knowing she got her ass handed to her by a blind girl.

Torch laughs and then I'm airborne for a second before he sets me on the motorcycle. I scoot back and slip on the leather jacket. After he sets the helmet on my head, I snap the straps to secure it. He climbs on and starts it up, his hands going to my thighs as he pulls me close until I am front to back with him.

Leaning my head to the side, I kiss his cheek and feel him smile. I pull back and smile before laying my head on his back as we roar out of the parking lot.

five

Kayla

Torch and I cuddle on the couch with his head in my lap before bed. I run my hands through his hair, feeling totally relaxed around this man. I don't think I have felt this at ease in my whole entire life with anyone, which is crazy since we just met. I may have a huge crush on him.

I lean forward and kiss his forehead. When I start to pull away, his hand grabs the back of my head and pulls me down until my lips are touching his. I wrap my teeth around his bottom lip and pull, teasing him.

He growls and tries to kiss me harder, but I pull back again. Just an inch away from his lips. I bite my lip and smile, knowing he will have enough of my teasing any second.

He pushes me off of him and down onto the couch, so I'm lying flat on my back. I laugh as his teeth nip at my sides, and put my hands into his hair, pulling the ends, hard. He hisses and slams his lips on mine.

His large, rough hand cups my jaw, controlling the kiss. He moves between my legs, and I wrap them around his waist, locking my feet together. His hand moves from my face and down to my thigh, holding me still. He grinds his dick against my short shorts. I break the kiss and throw my head back, gasping at the feel. He's freaking huge.

When he kisses down my neck, I turn my head to the side, basking in his touch. This man knows how to burn me alive!

"Torch," I gasp and raise my hips to grind against him harder. I need more.

"Yes," he growls against my ear and nips at the lobe.

"I need you," I moan as I rub myself against him. My orgasm is within reach, but I need more. I need him in such a way I never thought I would need a guy.

He stills completely then shifts against me. *What is he doing?* I ask myself.

I feel his face come to the side of my face again. "Then you have me," he whispers into my ear, making me shiver at his words.

His hands go to the waistband of my shorts and start tugging. I lift my hips so he can pull them down with ease. I may or may not be wearing panties right now. Hey, once I am home, I strip my bra and panties. I want to be comfortable; but it also means easy access.

Torch hisses in approval. His finger drags through my wet folds, and I clench at the feel, wanting those fingers to work their magic. I moan.

Torch gets completely off the couch. When I hear the zipper of his jeans, I bite my lip in anticipation. I don't know what he is doing or what he will do next, but I know I will be completely surprised, and it's thrilling.

I jump when his mouth latches onto my clit and sucks hard. I scream as I come unexpectedly over and over, my body shaking with the aftershocks. Holy shit.

As I catch my breath, I raise forward and reach for Torch, who is now sitting between my legs. I want more of him. No, I *need* more.

"I want you," I tell him breathlessly.

"Are you sure?" he asks with a growl in his voice.

I smile saucily, not even caring I may not be looking directly at him. "Positive."

His arms wrap around me, and I'm thrown over his shoulders. I laugh as he starts running up the stairs, my face hitting his back with his every step. Reaching my hand down, I pinch his butt and receive a smack on the ass in return.

The door creaks as he enters the bedroom, and then I'm thrown onto the bed. I lift my shirt over my head, leaving myself completely naked.

It's silent. The room is so silent I can hear my own breath. Feeling uneasy, I rub my hands together.

"You're beautiful."

I jerk in shock, not expecting his words. Multiple people have called me beautiful before, but it's different when he says it. Because I know he means it. Unable to help myself, I grin from ear-to-ear.

The bed moves as Torch climbs on top of it. His hand touches my arm then drags up to my shoulder. He pushes me down onto the bed, then his hands go to my legs then down to my shins, pulling them apart, baring me to him.

His finger touches my slit, and I gasp at the sudden feel. He presses a finger inside, then another. I moan at the feeling of being filled, as he leisurely moves them, and feel him curl the tips, hitting something inside me. Insane pleasure flows through me, and I moan.

"Oh God," I say over and over again.

"Last chance to back out," Torch says.

"Not a chance," I tell him and scoot farther up the bed. I hear the crinkle of the condom. His hands touch me as he moves up my body. Each of his hands stroke my cheekbones before he places them on the bed beside me. My hands hold on to each of his wrists.

His lips touch mine as I feel his dick touch my entrance. I suck in a sharp breath and run my hands up his arms and onto his shoulders, wrapping them around his neck. I feel him shift as he presses an inch in. He's freaking huge.

"More," I tell him breathlessly and bring one leg up to his butt, pressing him toward me. He pushes a couple more inches in, slowly letting me adjust. Nodding, I give him the go-ahead, and he slams all the way in.

I throw my head back. It's slightly painful. I'm also feeling incredibly full. Fuller than I thought possible. He's so big.

I feel his stomach press closer to mine and reach to either side of me. He is now on his elbows. I'm completely boxed in.

"Move."

That's all the encouragement he needs. He moves all the way out until only the tip is inside then slams all the way back in.

"Oh God," I scream at the intense feeling.

He does it again, and I raise my hips, meeting him thrust for thrust. Wanting, needing more. His hands grab mine and raise them above my head while his lips nip my neck and my breasts, driving me crazy.

"Harder!" I say through my moaning.

He does just as I ask, and I'm getting pushed up the bed until my hands hit the headboard. I hold on to it to keep from hitting my head.

My body stiffens as my orgasm comes closer and closer, the fire in the pit of my stomach turning into an inferno.

When Torch taps my clit, I scream at the top of my lungs as I come, the orgasm exploding through me.

Through my sex-induced fog, I hear Torch roar out his own orgasm before he lies on top of me with his face at the crook of my neck.

We lie together for a minute or so, trying to come back down from our high.

"Damn," I mutter.

Torch laughs and kisses my forehead tenderly. I slide my hand up his face and into his hair, where I grab a handful and pull him toward me, wanting a kiss. Torch takes my lead and kisses me back. This kiss is full of passion, making me want him all over again.

He sits up, breaking the kiss as he pulls out of me. He's really quiet, and I feel him stiffen. "What's wrong?"

"The condom broke."

"What?" I yell a little too loudly. "I'm not on any birth control."

"Oh, well," he says, surprising the shit out of me with his easy-going tone. *How is he not freaking out?*

"Huh?"

"If you get pregnant, then you just do."

Mind. Blown. I fall back onto the bed trying to wrap my head around this. I feel him get off the bed and put my arm across my eyes. What would I do if I got pregnant? I know I would try to be the best mother I could be, even if

Torch decides to not stick around. I don't feel like he would do that, though. He raised Paisley alone.

A wet cloth touches my pussy, scaring me. He's cleaning me. Holy shit. Is it bad that I almost start crying?

You could say that I have been deprived of touch for a long time. My mom wasn't always touchy feely, and my dad never touched me at all; unless it was by accident.

With Torch I never hesitated and behave exactly the opposite. I want his touch. Even with my ex, we would have sex, but that would be it. There were feelings attached; touching him felt wrong and made me feel uneasy. Torch makes me feel safe, and I want to soak that up.

He climbs into bed and wraps his arms around me from behind, spooning me. He kisses my cheek, and I can't help but smile. He is so sweet.

"It will all be okay, baby. No point stressing over it." He kisses the back of my head.

"I know." I place my hand on top of his hand and reach with my free hand to drag the blanket over us.

"Goodnight."

"Goodnight, baby."

Six

Kayla

Six weeks later

"I got it," Torch says, and the door slams behind him. What he got is a pregnancy test. I missed my period, and two weeks have gone past. It may just be stress, right?

I'm so freaking nervous that I can barely control myself. What if I am pregnant? I just met this guy seven weeks ago, and I may be pregnant. We haven't had any other accidents since the condom breaking during our first time together.

It's early in the morning, and I'm dying to pee. I grab a small plastic cup I'm going to pee in and put the test inside. Since I am blind as a bat, Torch will be the one to reveal the result.

Grabbing the boxes from him, I go into the bathroom and lock the door behind me. Knowing Torch, he will try to help me pee in the cup or something. Men. Since he knew about the possibility of me being pregnant, Torch has watched my every step.

The past couple of weeks with Torch have been amazing. We had a lot of hot sex, and I have to admit I'm really starting to care for him; I do more so every single day.

Pulling down my pants, I pee into the cup then stick the test inside for a few seconds before I set it on the sink. I pour the pee in the toilet before I throw the cup away. I know this house like the back of my hand now.

I unlock the door then close the back of the toilet seat to sit on it. The door opens and Torch touches my shoulder. I turn around and lay my head against his abs, breathing in his scent.

The next few minutes are torture as I gnaw on my bottom lip nervously. "I'm going to check now," Torch says, and I hold my breath as he moves away from me.

"You're pregnant."

Those two words just changed my whole entire life. I'm going to be a mother. A sob escapes, and I lift my hand to my mouth, trying to hold them in.

When Torch lifts me off the toilet, my legs go around his waist while my head rests on his shoulder as I cry, because my heart is filled with such joy even though this is so unexpected. Hell, my life has been turned upside down in such a short amount of time.

"Shh, baby. Don't cry," he soothes and kisses the top of my head. Lifting my head, I kiss him and hold his face between my hands. I can't help but cry a little as I kiss him. I feel him shake with emotion, too.

Pulling away, I wipe away my tears, and he kisses my temple to bring that smile out of me with his sweetness.

"You're mine," Torch says in a gruff voice as his hand tightens on my hips.

"What?"

"You heard me. You're going to wear my patch. You are my woman," he repeats, and I break into a smile again, feeling totally fine with that idea.

Torch starts walking, and I know he's entering the bedroom. I'm laid gently onto the bed and stripped out of my clothes. He pushes me against the bed and kisses my knees, up to my hips, and stops at my belly button, where he presses a kiss as he holds each side of my stomach. I can't hold back the tears that fall at the feel of him touching me in such a tender, sweet way.

"My son, you will be loved. I can't wait to meet you." He lays his head on my stomach.

Unable to help myself, I cry silently, my heart heavy with emotion. I can blame it on hormones.

Torch glides up my body and eases inside me gently. I widen my legs. His hand glides down my side. He moves inside of me slowly, and I moan. This feeling is beyond any other time we've been together.

That's when I notice he isn't wearing a condom.

The next hour Torch spends worshiping my body and setting me on fire.

Since it's still early in the morning, Torch calls and manages to get me an appointment at the gynecologist.

I get dressed and can feel him hovering. He won't even let me reach up onto the shelf to get a shirt off the rack without doing it for me. Hell, when I bend over to put my pants on, he doesn't like that either and stops me to put them on halfway for me. If he is like this the whole entire pregnancy, I'm doomed and may just kill him.

I walk out of the bedroom and toward the steps, but when I am picked up off the ground, I sigh in frustration.

"Why are you doing this?" I ask him, hoping he will get the hint and stop hovering.

"You may fall," he says and then carries me right out of the house. I know because of the drastic temperature change.

The truck door opens and I'm set inside. He climbs inside and buckles me up. As soon as he shuts the door, I laugh incredulously at this man.

"You tell your mom yet?" he asks, and I am assuming he means telling her about the pregnancy.

"Nope," I answer simply, hoping he will leave it at that.

I am bitter and more so now. Even this early into the pregnancy I would do anything in my power to protect this baby inside of me.

"You know, you never told me why you don't talk to your mother."

I feel us going around a curve and rest my head against the window, wanting to talk about anything but this. "I had a rough childhood, and my mom did nothing to stop it."

"Baby, I know you don't want to tell me. I won't pressure you, because I don't want you to be stressed out."

I let out a huge breath, relieved the disaster is averted. I know bringing up old memories won't be good for me.

We pull up in front of the doctor's office. I don't bother trying to get out of the vehicle, because I have tried multiple times, and every time Torch had a hissy fit; but I have to admit, I secretly like his alphaness, since I write about men like him.

Torch leads me with a hand at the small of my back as we walk inside of the building, the cold, air-conditioned air hitting us in the face. He leads me over to a desk I am assuming, since my hand touches a counter.

I notice the room is completely silent around us, and it was filled with noise before. Hmm, weird. Torch wraps his arm around me with his hand holding my stomach. I place my hand on top of his.

"Fill out these papers and bring them back to me."

Torch leads us over to some seats, and I sit down. The pen scratches on the papers as he fills them out. I guess I can't be of much help, since I can't see.

"Let me take these papers back," he tells me, and the seat creaks as he gets up. I scoot farther back into the seat.

"You're one lucky bitch," a voice says from beside me, and I jump, not expecting it.

"What do you mean?" I ask the voice whose owner is now touching me.

"Is that your old man?" she asks and wraps her fingers around my wrist, squeezing slightly. I swear if she doesn't quit touching me, I'm going to backhand her.

"Yeah," I draw out, wanting her to get to the point. I hear her sigh loudly. She grips my wrist tighter, her fingernails digging in. "Those men protect their women with their life and all but worship the ground they walk on; and heaven forbid if someone dares to hurt them or their kids."

Hot dang. I knew Torch was a different breed all together, but the whole MC is like that? I hear Torch's footsteps as he walks back to me, and the girl squeezes my wrist even tighter.

"Let go of me." I pull on my wrist, and she lets go. I pull my arm away from her, not wanting to give her the chance to touch me again. Why must people think it's okay to always touch me?

Torch sits down beside me and pulls me into his side. His hand wraps around my back and touches my belly.

"Why is that girl staring at you?" he whispers into my ear.

"She's an MC groupie." I shrug my shoulders.

He chuckles under his breath and kisses the top of my head. Goodness, he is so freaking sweet I can't get over it.

"We have a party at the club tonight. I'll be introducing you as my ole lady."

I nod, "All right."

"I like this agreeable side of you," he teases, and I elbow him in the side. "Watch yourself, buddy, or I just may be disagreeable through this whole pregnancy."

"Kayla McIntosh!" The nurse shouts. I stand up, and Torch follows the nurse, leading me as we walk for a few seconds.

The next thirty minutes are filled with peeing in a cup and the nurse checking all of my vitals, and now I am sitting on a bed in a room, wearing one of those awful hospital gowns that don't even try to cover my butt as they don't have a back.

I hear the door open and am assuming the doctor walks in. "You are indeed pregnant. But I think you already knew that," the male voice says. I take a deep breath knowing that what will happen next won't be good.

I laugh slightly and twist my hands in my lap. Torch's hand tightens in mine. "First, we are going to do an internal ultrasound, and then we need to do a Pap smear. I need you to lie down on the bed and spread your legs." His voice is giving me the creeps. I gulp and lie down on the bed, wishing I could fucking see what's happening right now.

Then I remember the nurse saying she was going to schedule me for a Pap in a week or so. "The nurse said she was going to schedule me for that later."

"We will just get it over with today." His tone is dismissing me.

I bite my lip, while my gut is telling me to leave. I don't like the vibes I am getting. I hear plastic hitting against each other and get nervous. Then there's the click of a bottle opening. Then I hear the doctor's footsteps as he comes closer to me, and I start to panic, not knowing what exactly is about to happen.

"Wait. You mean that has to go up her?" Torch asks, a bit of anger in his voice, which scares me even more.

"Yes, until she is farther along, we have to conduct ultrasounds this way," he explains, as I feel him touch the inside of my leg. I jump and start to panic. Torch touches his forehead to mine, and I instantly calm down considerably.

He puts the wand up me. It's really, really uncomfortable. He moves it around inside me with hard, jerky movements. I flinch as it hits my cervix.

I hear him clicking buttons and then hear the sound of my baby's heartbeat in the room. Tears come to my eyes at the sound. I'm going to be a mom; it just hit me.

"You just made me the happiest man in the world." Torch presses a kiss on my lips.

"You're six weeks along," the doctor says, interrupting our moment, and then pulls the wand out and snaps off his gloves. *Why is he taking them off? I don't want him to touch me without gloves.*

"You better have gloves on," I call him out and feel Torch sit up.

"I-I-I was just about to put a new pair on," the doctor stutters, and I know I just caught the man red-handed about to touch me without gloves. I can only imagine how many girls he has done this to.

"Babe, get your clothes on." Torch helps me up from the bed then down onto the ground before he places my clothes in my hand. The bathroom is attached to this room, so he turns me in the right direction. As I close the door, I hear a loud thump.

Torch

The doctor is a freaking dead man. He is staring at me looking like he is about to piss his pants, as he should. He was ready to touch Kayla without gloves on, and we all know the reason why.

I stalk toward him, while he backs away with his hands held up in surrender. I grab him by the throat and push him against the wall hard. I hear the bathroom door click and look down at the doctor.

"You just messed with the wrong fucking woman. She is my ole lady, and you just got on the shit side of the Devil's Soul MC." I press my hand into his neck hard, making him gasp for air. "Do you know what that means?" I ask and smile down at him. He shakes his head no. "You just made your life a living hell. If you had touched her, you would already be dead." His eyes widen and his fat jaw shakes from his head shaking back and forth.

When I release him, he almost hits the floor. I raise my hand and hit him on the shoulder, hard. "Watch your back."

Hearing something splash on the floor, I look down and see the guy is pissing himself. I laugh at him. Pussy.

Kayla comes out of the bathroom with her hand slightly in front of her. She looks up and looks me straight in the face even though she doesn't know she is doing so. She is so fucking gorgeous.

"You ready to go?" I start in her direction.

"Oh, I forgot my phone in the bathroom." She turns around and hesitantly walks back into the bathroom.

I turn around and look at the doctor, catching him staring at Kayla. That fucking asshole is just trying to die. Growling, I walk over, grab him by the back of the head, and smash his head against the sink. He collapses to the floor. "I-I will call the police," he cries out.

I laugh in his face. "Yeah, fucker, go to the police. Guess whose friends with everyone on the force."

I smell the stench of shit. Well, I will be damned. The fucker shit his pants. It's been a while since that's happened.

"I'm ready," Kayla says, and I walk over and pick her up, not wanting her to step in the man's piss. She wraps her legs around me and holds on tight. I see her twitch her nose. "Something smells horrible in here."

I laugh, and the doctor makes a choked noise. "I do believe the doctor shit his pants."

Her mouth pops open and shuts a couple times before she throws her head back laughing. I set her back onto the ground once we're outside of the room. She continues laughing, holding her stomach.

We walk back into the waiting room, and people stare at her. But *my* Kayla doesn't care. She is laughing even harder now and barely able to walk. Rolling my eyes, I pick her up off the ground and carry her bridal style.

"You all right?" I ask once I set her in the truck. She wipes her eyes and breathes in and out deeply.

"You made the guy shit himself, didn't you?" She grins from ear-to-ear, that dimple on her right cheek popping out.

"Yeah." I chuckle and buckle her up before I close her door and walk over to my side of the truck, hop in, and shut the door before I put the key in the ignition and fire up the air conditioner.

"It makes me wonder, Torch. What do you look like?" She is still laughing slightly.

"I have tattoos covering both of my arms' full sleeves, my hair is longer on top, but shorter on the sides, I have a five o'clock shadow, am 6'3 and 240 pounds of muscle, and my eyes are dark brown." I tell her the basics of what I look like and see her face darken with a sexy look, which means she is turned on. "What's that look for?"

"You have full sleeves?" she asks and puts her hair up in a bun thing on top of her head.

"Yeah."

Her head shoots in my direction. "Oh. My. God. I am dating a freaking bad boy and didn't even know it!" She fans herself dramatically.

"You're such a little shit." I laugh at her dramatics.

"I'm *your* little shit, though." Her voice turns husky, and she smiles a shit-eating grin.

"That's right, and you're not going anywhere."

Kayla

First off, I am dating a tattooed badass, which makes my girly bits ready to combust. All girls have a thing for bad boys. Torch is a part of an MC, rides a motorcycle, and apparently can make a man shit his pants.

Any sane person would run from a man who can make a guy shit himself, but I'm not sane. And to be honest, him being a bad boy makes him a million times more attractive to me.

"Baby, we're going to the clubhouse. Your leather is on the seat beside you."

I reach over until my hand touches a leather vest. I pick it up and put it on. "What does it say?"

"Property of Torch." I can hear the smugness in his voice and can't help but feel thrilled at him claiming me in such a caveman way. I love his caveman ways. What girl wouldn't?

He pulls to a stop and gets out of the truck, then slams his door shut and mine opens a second later. He grabs me by the waist and lifts me out of the truck, takes my hand, and I follow him. I realize in this moment how much I fully trust this man. I should be scared giving myself fully like this to him, but I'm not. He hasn't given me one reason to second-guess him, so I'm not going to start now.

"Step."

I step up and hear a door open then loud talking, which once we enter, stops. It gets so quiet that you could hear a pin drop. I bite my lip nervously, because it feels like there are a million eyes on me.

"This is my ole lady, Kayla, and she is knocked up!" Torch yells into the room, and my heart literally stops. Holy. Shit. I didn't expect this.

I hear feet stomping and men yelling. Women squealing. And then a woman wraps me into a hug, unless guys wear womans perfume.

"I'm so happy for you guys! I'm Jean," she says while still hugging me. I grin at this woman who is so bubbly.

"Thank you!"

She pulls away and kisses me on the cheek. Then she grabs my hand and pulls me away. I'm not sure she knows I'm blind. "I'm blind." Blunt and straightforward is how I roll.

"Oh, I know," she says softly and leads me farther away from Torch. "You need to meet the other ole ladies. The hoovers are in the corner over there sulking at you."

"Hoovers?" I ask, confused.

"Oh, the hang-arounds. They want to be ole ladies, but the men don't want them. They never get the idea, and you just took a guy off the market," she explains, and I lift my hand in the direction of the skanks and flip them off. They'll think twice about sulking at me again.

I hear Torch's booming laugh from behind me and know I'm caught. *Oops.*

"Oh. My. Goodness. I just fell in love with you!" Jean says through her own laughter, and then everyone in the room starts laughing with her and Torch.

"Bitch!" I hear someone scream. That best not be directed at me.

Jean cackles evilly, and then I hear the lady that yelled at me scream. "What's going on?"

"Oh, she's getting thrown out. You don't disrespect ole ladies in the club. They are held in the highest honor."

"Wow." I knew being an ole lady was a special thing in the club, but I didn't realize how special.

"Here in front of you is Chrystal. She is with the president of the club. She also runs the women's center."

I raise my hand in front of me, and she grabs it, shaking it. "Nice to meet the woman who brought Torch to his knees." She chuckles, and then I feel her arms around my neck hugging me.

"Ha-ha, that man drives me the best kind of crazy," I tell her as she pulls back.

Another set of arms wrap around me. "I'm Tiffany. I am also an ole lady." I hug her back and smile.

"Hi, I'm Darcy! I am a gynecologist. Torch told me I'm needed?" A voice says beside me.

"Umm, yeah, I'm going to need to find a new one. Torch made the one I saw today shit himself." I grimace at the memory of the smell.

"Shit himself?" Jean asks incredulously.

"Yeah, the doctor insisted on doing a Pap, and I heard him take off his gloves. I called him out on it, knowing he was going to touch me with his bare hands." I shift my feet at the girls' silence. I know what the guy could've done would have been horrible.

"Oh my God!" Jean gasps and wraps me in another hug.

"What doctor was it?" Bell asks in a strange voice.

"Doctor Cornett."

She gasps loudly. "What's the matter?" I ask her and move in the direction of her gasp.

"I just saw him a week ago and felt weird when he was touching me down there. When he went toward the sink, I noticed he didn't have gloves on, but I thought he already took them off." She starts crying. I know how she feels. Violated.

"Bell! What's the matter?" A man yells. His feet are hitting the cement floor as he runs over.

I feel a large hand touch my back and know instantly it's Torch. "What's the matter, baby?" the man soothes Bell. She tells him what happened to me, then what happened to her.

Torch wraps his arm around me. It's killing me. She is still crying, and my heart is breaking for her. Turning in Torch's arms, I lay my head on his chest, feeling like crying myself.

"Church!" A man yells, and I hear chairs scooting back and heavy footsteps walking out of the room.

"I'll be back." Torch kisses the top of my head before he walks out of the room.

"Shh, baby. I have you, and this fucker will pay." Bell's man soothes her, and I hear her sniff. "I have to go to church."

"Okay," she whispers and then arms are wrapped around me again. Wet cheeks hit my neck. Bell. I hug her tightly, letting her cry as much as she needs to. I hate this so fucking much.

Later that night, I lie in bed with Torch. He's behind me, holding me close. He was in church or a meeting with the club for an hour. Bell settled down a little bit after that, but kept holding on to me. Her whole body was shaking until her husband came back and made her feel safe, telling her everything would be okay.

Paisley is coming in for the weekend, so I get to meet Torch's daughter. He already told her about me, but I am feeling incredibly nervous. Who wouldn't be? I'm meeting my man's kid for the first time ever. What if she doesn't like me?

Tomorrow night is Thursday. Jean and the rest of the ole ladies are having a girls' night. Well, since half of us are knocked up, it's going to be a movie and dinner. I feel damn old now, 'cause my night out consists of food and a movie.

Torch moves in his sleep and rests his hand on my stomach. All day his hand kept moving to touch it. I close my eyes. I need to get some sleep. Today has been beyond exhausting.

seven

"Oh my God, girl! Do you even know how hot your man is?" Jean gasps and clutches onto my arm like I'm her lifeline.

"Well, I guess not," I tell her feeling amused, and by her reaction I'm assuming he is smokin'.

"Girl, if you saw how many girls drool over him, you'd be ready to kick ass twenty-four seven, though poor ole Torch has his work cut out for him, too. You walk into a room and men stop what they're doing to stare at you."

"Thank you, I guess." I laugh at her and take a drink of my water. Jean is growing on me with her peppy, super-happy attitude.

"How far along are you?" Bell asks from my other side.

"Six weeks." I take a bite of my steak.

"I'm three months," she says happily. I'm glad she is doing better after what happened yesterday.

"Hey, ladies. Would you guys like a drink?" a male voice asks from directly in front of us.

"No, thank you. We're fine," Chrystal tells him.

"Come on!" the dude says, and Jean's shoulder hits mine hard.

"What the fuck are you doing, dickwad?" she asks. I feel her body move again, hitting my shoulder.

"Just scoot over," the dude says.

I'm not in the fucking mood to deal with this fucker. "Listen here, dipshit, you have ten fucking seconds to get out of my face, or my taser is about to fry some dick." I reach down into my purse, pull my taser out, and wag it in his direction.

"I'm sorry. I just wanted to hang out," he whines like the fucking pussy he is.

"Yeah, well, when a lady says no it means no. Now, get up and let me eat in peace. Never mess with a hungry pregnant lady." I click the button so he can hear the crackling sound.

Then I hear a huge racket and retreating footsteps. I sigh and stick my taser back into my purse. Grabbing my fork, I take another bite of my steak. I wasn't lying. I am damn hungry.

"If I were a lesbian, I would so bang the shit out of you," Jean says in awe. The rest of the girls start cracking up. I grin at all of them then get back to cleaning my plate.

"Well, here comes the fucking hoover the club kicked out yesterday," Bell whines beside me, and I bang my head against the wall.

"Well, well. It didn't fucking take long for the ole ladies to welcome you into the club," she sneers. An intense smell of French whore hits me. Gah, why must she wear dollar-store perfume? I think my nose hairs are burnt off.

"You best not be talking to me, girl," I warn her without turning my head from my food.

"I am, bitch! I was kicked out of the club," she wails in her fake baby voice that irks my nerves. I ignore her and continue to eat.

"Remember who had him first!" she taunts cockily and cackles like the evil bitch she is.

I look up at that and grin from ear-to-ear. Does she honestly think I am falling for that?

"What are you smiling at?" she asks snootily.

"You. You honestly think I am going to get mad over that? I know you didn't fuck him, because no man in the fucking club would touch you or your cronies. You're hang-arounds. I knew he wasn't a virgin before he met me, but that doesn't matter now, because I'm his ole lady and you will continue being a whore who spreads her legs for anything that has a dick. Have a little respect for yourself and maybe a man will show the same respect for you. Now, go fucking sit down before I whip out my taser and fry your face."

"I-I-I," she stutters, then her heels clack on the ground as she walks away.

"Ha! I got it on record this time!" Bell laughs and wraps an arm around me, hugging me.

"What is it tonight? Fuck with Kayla night?" I sigh and sit back in my seat rubbing my belly.

"Get her!" Jean yells again out loud in the theater. We are watching *Tarzan*. Well, they are watching while I am listening. The movie is coming to an end, and I'm not sure what the hell is happening now, because their voices don't explain what's going on.

A few minutes later, it ends and Chrystal leads me out of the theater. "Here comes Torch."

I can't stop the grin that crosses my face. My man is here. His hand touches mine and I plow into his stomach, hugging him and moving from side to side. I lift my face toward him. "Missed you."

"Missed you, too, baby." He kisses me on the lips.

"Have you been a bad girl?" he teases.

I suck my lips into my mouth. "Maybe."

A hand smacks me on the butt. "Naughty girl. I think I'll punish you." He chuckles as he leads me to his truck. No more motorcycle until I pop the baby out.

I sit in the middle of the bench seat on the way home. I have really missed him, because we usually spend every evening together.

He lifts my hand and kisses the back of it. My heart skips a beat. This man is too much to handle sometimes. He gets my emotions all out of whack. I'm falling fast for him.

Once we enter the house, I am slammed up against the wall, Torch's lips on mine. I sink my hands into his hair and pull at the ends. He rips my shirt over my head and pushes my leggings down. They are thrown across the room with my underwear.

His hand fists my hair and pulls so my neck is exposed. He bites it, his teeth skimming my skin. Two fingers move between my folds and into my pussy. I moan and pull Torch tighter against me.

I hear his belt then his pants hit the floor. He lifts me off the ground, my back hitting the wall, his cock at my entrance. All it would take is one small movement for him to be inside. "Ahh!" I scream at the sudden fullness.

Torch doesn't move for a few moments, letting me adjust. I lock my feet behind his back and hold on for the ride. We have fucked more times than I can count, but this is different. Torch has fully unleashed, and I'm loving it.

My body feels like it's on fire, and he's fucking me harder. "Oh my god!" I put my hands on the wall behind my head trying to find something to keep myself tethered. The fire in my stomach becomes unbearable. My toes curl.

Throwing my head back, I scream as I come, the spasms hitting me over and over again. I feel Torch fill me up and then come to a stop. I fall forward, my head on his shoulder, unable to move and not sure I'll be able to again after this.

He carries me up the stairs. I hear the shower come on before he opens the glass door and steps in, the spray hitting my back. I don't bother moving my head from his shoulder, because the orgasm took the life out of me.

Torch washes my body, and I hug him tighter to me. I don't know what I would do without this man now that I have him in my life. He has become such an important part and has consumed every section of my mind.

He washes my body and himself then we climb into bed. I turn onto my side and he wraps his arm around me, his hand on my stomach.

"I can't wait to meet my son." He kisses the back of my head.

"How do you know it's a boy?"

"I just know. I knew with Paisley," he explains while he rubs my still flat stomach.

I want to be the best mother I can possibly be, because it's something I didn't have. I want my kids to be kids and grow up being happy. I don't want them to worry about their next meal or if someone will hurt them in the middle of the night.

"I promise to be the best mother I possibly can."

"I know, baby. You'll be a damn good mother."

I smile at his words.

Yawning, I walk down the stairs and turn into the living room. "What time will Paisley be here, Torch?"

"Hi, I'm Paisley," a sweet voice says, and I gape into nothing.

Holy shit, I am wearing nothing but her father's shirt. What a nice freaking first impression. She probably thinks I'm a whore.

"I-I...nice to meet you." I smile and point over my shoulder. "Let me go get some clothes on." I turn around and run back up the stairs.

I hurry into our room and slip on some jeans and a clean t-shirt before I walk back down the stairs into the living room. Torch wraps his arms around me from behind.

"Paisley, come here," Torch says, and I hear the chair creak as she stands up. I hold my breath. I didn't expect to be meeting her this early. I thought I had all day to prepare.

"Baby girl, meet Kayla. Kayla, meet Paisley," he introduces us and pushes me forward a little bit. My hand touches her shoulder and I step forward wrapping her in a tight hug. I'm not usually a hugger like this, but I felt the urge to hug her.

Torch

Her head touches my shoulder, and I notice her shoulders are shaking. My eyes widen. Did I do something wrong? "What's the matter?"

"Thank you for making my dad happy. I haven't seen him like this before. He always took care of me and never worried about his own happiness."

"Baby," Torch says softly, then she is taken from my arms. A tear slips free. Dang these pregnancy hormones.

"All right, enough with the sadness. Let me get to know Kayla, Dad. Go do manly things." She makes a shooing noise, and I hear him chuckle. She grabs my hand and leads me over to the couch, where I sit down with Paisley beside me.

"So you're pregnant?" she asks.

"Yeah." I grin and rub my stomach.

"Oh lord. I'm surprised Dad lets you walk. Whenever I got a cold, Dad wouldn't even let me walk half of the time." She laughs and I join in. That does sound like Torch.

"That's your dad. He drives me the best kind of crazy." I sit back farther into the couch and curl my feet up in the cushion. "How do you like college?"

"I like it! I miss Dad something fierce, though. We spent a lot of time together at the end after..." She stops and clears her throat. I know she is thinking about her getting attacked outside of her school.

"It's okay. I know what happened." I reach forward and search for her hand then take it in mine and give her a squeeze.

"I've never been so scared in my life. I was walking outside waiting for Dad to pick me up from school when I was tackled and thrown onto the ground." She stops again and clears her throat. My heart is breaking for her. Nobody should have to ever feel like this.

"He started ripping my clothes off, while I was fighting him with everything I had. Liam stopped him before it could get anywhere, but that feeling of helplessness is something I don't want to ever feel again."

"I'm so sorry," I say softly and wrap my arms around her. "You are more than what happened to you. You are more than all of it. Don't let it control your life, because that means he would be winning. You are a strong, beautiful woman." I kiss the top of her head. What's happened to me? I used to never be this touchy feely.

"Thank you for talking to me," she whispers. "I'm not usually this open about things."

"I'm never this touchy." I laugh and she does, too.

The weekend was spent with us getting to know each other. Torch let us have our own space so we could bond. I've grown attached to the girl over the weekend. She is so freaking sweet and has such a beautiful soul.

"You did an amazing job raising her, Torch," I tell him as we lie on the couch an hour after she left.

"Thank you. Raising a daughter was one of the hardest things I ever did. Having to explain *everything* to her. Something a dad shouldn't ever have to do." He laughs at the last part and I join him, envisioning Torch explaining the birds and the bees.

Torch

He turns on the TV and I cuddle up to him with my head on his shoulder. Closing my eyes, I listen to the sound of the TV.

eight

Kayla

I wake up to Torch's mouth on me. I moan and put my hand on top of his head, holding him tighter.

He shakes off my hand and moves up my body until his dick is at my entrance. I buck my hips hoping he will slip inside, which causes his dick to hit my asshole, and I scream like a little girl, "Exit only!"

Torch falls over to the side laughing his ass off, and I join along. Hey, I'm just not an anal girl. Placing my hand on Torch's shoulder, I push him flat onto his back, then move my legs to either side of him, straddling him.

Grabbing his dick, I slip him inside and moan. He feels even bigger and deeper this way. I put both of my hands on his chest and start rocking. Torch holds me at my hips, helping me move.

I move quicker and quicker until I am too tired to. Torch stops me and pulls me down until I am lying belly to belly with him. I feel him shift underneath me as both of his arms wrap around my back, anchoring me to him.

He flexes his hips, moving harder and harder until I am almost permanently screaming. I come again and again. With every movement he is hitting that same spot over and over again. "Torch!" I scream trying to do something to get rid of that burning fire that continues to get hotter even though I have come twice already.

"Torch, I can't take it!" I tell him and bite his arm.

He lets go with one arm, flicks my clit, and slams home.

"Ahhh!" I come again on a scream, my whole body shakes with spasms I can't control.

"Kayla!" Torch groans and moves one more time. He fills me full of his seed, my pussy milking him of everything he has while I am still going through the aftershocks.

He slips out of me, but I hang on tight to him, our hearts beating in unison, his hands running down my back.

"Holy shit. I think I actually died for a bit there," I tell Torch and let out a deep breath. I move my hair over my shoulder. "When can we do it again?"

He busts out laughing and kisses the top of my head tenderly. Damn those fucking butterflies. This man...I swear. He's just made to mess with my freaking emotions.

"Want to hang out with the girls at the club today?"

"Sure. When?" I yawn and snuggle into his chest.

"Thirty minutes."

I climb off of him and off the bed. I stretch raising my arms above my head, naked as the day I was born. "Don't put your arms above your head!" Torch yells and grabs them to put them down to my sides, ruining my stretch.

"Maybe you should take a bath instead of shower. Wait, I'll just fucking carry you." He picks me up off the ground so my legs are wrapped around him.

"You are not serious, right?"

"Deadly."

"I'm going to go crazy." I bang my head against his shoulder. He is going to drive me insane.

"Put me down, Torch." I wiggle in his arms, but he smacks my ass.

"Quit moving or I'll spank you."

I grin. "Promise?"

Torch growls and kisses me hard on the mouth. "You'll be the death of me."

"Nah, I think I already died three times today from orgasms. So, more than likely you'll be the one killing me," I tease as I tug the ends of his hair. He sets me on my feet once we enter the shower. "But what a good way to go."

He laughs and stands on the other side of the shower. His shower is super huge and has two showerheads. I get busy washing my hair, shaving, the works.

"Hurry your ass up, woman." Torch smacks my ass and steps out of the shower. Rolling my eyes, I mutter to myself, "Men."

We pull up in front of the club. I hear the rattle of the gate as it closes behind us. Torch opens my door and has his hands around my waist when we hear gunshots hitting something metal around us with a ping.

I scream and Torch pushes me flat down on the seat with his body on top of mine

I hear more gunshots and a man yell.

Then motorcycles leaving the clubhouse.

Then dead silence.

My whole body is shaking. I can't believe we just got fucking shot at.

"Shh, baby, you're okay," Torch soothes me. He picks me up, and we are out of the truck. He runs with me in his arms. Cold air hits me as we enter the clubhouse. I hear men yelling and the door slamming shut as they leave the room.

"Baby, I need to go catch these men. You and the other ole ladies are going to ground until we get back. Nobody can get in. Hell, this building can be on fire and you guys wouldn't be affected. Prospects will be outside the door."

I nod knowing stuff like this will happen; it's part of the MC. He leads me somewhere, and I hear a big metal sound as a door opens.

"Kayla!" Jean screams and folds me into her arms.

"Get in, girls," Kyle says, and Jean leads me into another room. More arms wrap around me. The door slams closed and I hear beeping noises like someone is pressing buttons.

"We're locked in. Get those fuckers," Chrystal says. I can hear how pissed she is.

"You okay, girl?" Jean asks and hugs me again.

"I will be okay. My nerves are fucking shot. I was just shot at," I tell her and pull back. I sit back in my chair, letting out a deep breath, trying to relax.

I'm scared for Torch. He is out there trying to catch those guys. I don't want him hurt. I love that man with everything in me. He has wiggled his way into my heart and is now holding it in his clutches.

"They will be fine, honey. Someone is fucking brave doing this, especially at the compound. Mercy will not be shown," Chrystal reassures me. I can hear the hardness in her voice. This woman is the club mother, and she is pissed someone messed with her kids.

We all sit and wait. Wondering what is happening, if they are okay. When will they be back?

Torch

Once the girls are locked underground, me and Kyle run up the stairs going after those fuckers that dared to try and hurt us. The look of fear on Kayla's face will be something that won't happen again if I can help it.

We climb on our motorcycles and roar out of the club's parking lot. Prospects are at the gate, armed. We need to fucking bulletproof the gate so people can't shoot through the rails. The clubhouse is surrounded by fucking brick walls.

Some of the brothers in the parking lot piled out of the lot as soon as those fuckers quit shooting. Rage doesn't come close to what I am feeling right now. Someone attempted to hurt what is mine, and that someone is going to hurt, bad.

All twenty of us are roaring up the highway; cars are pulling to the side of the road knowing not to fuck with us. Five of our brothers are ahead of us tailing the fuckers.

For the next ten minutes, we fly up the highway until we see our brothers on the side of the road with three other motorcycles. They caught the fuckers. We pull in next to our brothers' bikes and surround the other motorcycles.

We all get off our bikes when I hear a loud piercing whistle, the sign the guys have them. I grin evilly; it's time to fucking deliver some pain.

We all go into the woods and up ahead see Ryan, Techy, Butch, Trey, and Vin standing watch over all three of the men on their knees with their hands behind their heads.

Butch looks up at us grinning that sick-as-fuck smile. His name is Butch, because he likes to cut shit up. You don't want on the fucker's bad side, and these guys just messed with a whole lot of people he cares about.

Trey has his gun trained on the smaller guy's temple, grinding it in. The guy's lip is trembling and I can see a dark stain covering the front of his pants. The fucker already pissed himself.

Ryan is the enforcer and is a weapon of mass of destruction. One punch and you're laid the fuck out. He is an ex-SEAL and can kill you a million fucking ways.

Techy's name makes him sound like a geek, but he's far from it with his 6'4 and him being ex-Special Forces. He always keeps that shit-eating grin on his face, like right now.

"Well, well, what do we have here?" I taunt and move closer to the men on the ground.

"You got the wrong guys," the one that pissed himself says, and I notice the fucking tattoo covering the side of his neck and face.

"Kyle, look at his face."

Kyle steps around me. His eyes widen in anger. The next town over has the same gang we got rid of here.

"Check him for wires," Kyle orders. I grin knowing shit is about to get real. Ryan checks them over and nods to Kyle.

"Butch, gag them," Kyle tells Butch, who grins.

"Prospect, get my torch."

All three of the guys' eyes snap to mine. *Yeah, fuckers, look into my eyes. The eyes of the man who is about to kill your asses.*

The torch is put into my hand. Kyle nods at me. He's giving me this, because I was outside in the lot when those fuckers were shooting.

The next few minutes are filled with the smell of burning skin and the screams of those fuckers while they're giving us everything they know about the gang they are associated with. Then Kyle puts the silencer on his gun, and I stick it to their foreheads one by one, pulling the trigger as I go.

Everyone who knows the most sacred rule of the Devil's Soul MC is you don't mess with the ole ladies, because death will be hell for you; the whole wrath of the MC will come down on your ass.

We all have been trained to kill and protect. If we weren't, do you think Kyle would have let us in?

"Acid the bodies then dump them all but him." Kyle points at the big one.

"Techy, plant a bomb on his chest. Butch, you help him and drive a damn truck through the fucking building. Bomb the fucking place down. No one is going to survive. This threat is going to get answered."

"Got it, boss," Techy says, while Butch nods his head. They get to work while the rest of the guys head back to the compound.

People may wonder what would happen if we got caught by the police. Who do you think is in whose pocket? They are in ours. We don't fuck with people unless they screw with our ole ladies, and the men on the force couldn't give two shits. They turn the other way as long as men like that aren't out on their streets.

The fuckers are dead and won't be a threat to Kayla anymore. The whole gang is going up in flames. I do what I do to protect my family and have no regrets doing that.

The fucker that attempted to rape my daughter was killed and dumped as well. The whole entire club was involved in that. Those men helped raise my baby girl.

I watch as Locke pours sugar in these guys' motorcycles. Why the fuck does he have that on him? Shaking my head, I climb on my bike, and we all drive back to the compound to break our girls out of the ground.

Kayla

An hour later, I hear the door open. "It's safe to go out now," Chrystal says.

Jean leads me out of the room and up the stairs that lead back into the clubhouse. We walk inside the main room when I hear men talking all around, including Torch. I almost collapse onto the floor knowing he is okay.

"Torch," I call out wanting to hold him and make sure he is truly here. Then he has me in his arms. I let out the breath I was holding waiting for my man.

"I was scared you would be hurt," I tell him and he kisses me on the mouth. I take all of him in, reassuring myself he is here.

"I'm not and I'm okay."

I don't say anything back, but instead hug him to me, not wanting him to be in danger like that. I know it's a part of the whole MC thing, but that doesn't make it any easier.

I realize how easy it is for someone to be taken out of your life. Torch has become everything to me.

I love him.

Love doesn't wait for you to accept it. Love has no time.

nine

Kayla

Why the fuck is my phone ringing? Groaning, I roll over and grab it from the nightstand beside the bed and press the button. "Hello?" I yawn and fall back down onto the bed. Torch is awake rubbing my stomach.

"Hey, honey."

"Mom?" I sit up straight in bed. I haven't heard from her in a while.

"Honey, can I come stay with you for a while?" I hear her voice tremble. Something bad must have happened if she is asking this.

"What's wrong?" I ask. My hands start to shake.

"Your dad beat me up and I can't..."

I close my eyes and bite my lip. It's so fucking sad that she would leave him now, but not when I was a kid.

"You can stay in my apartment. I don't stay there anymore," I tell her. There's no way she is staying around me, because I don't want to be around my dad. My heart skips a beat at the thought. I haven't seen him since I was eleven.

"Kayla, what's wrong?" Torch urges at seeing my expression. He takes the phone from me and barks into the phone. "Who the fuck is this?"

Pause as he listens.

"We will be there in a couple of hours." He hangs up the phone.

"Baby, you need to tell me everything."

Sighing in resignation, I sit down Indian style on the bed. "I had a bad childhood. Your father is supposed to be your protector, but it seemed like mine just wanted me to suffer. I was locked into my bedroom for hours upon hours. He would change the furniture around in the house so I would purposely get hurt. I would sleep while rats he put there would crawl over me." I shudder at the thought. "He would hit me with things and I wouldn't see it coming." My life was hell, more so because I was blind. It got to the point I crawled wherever I could in the house; at least that way I wasn't so defenseless. My mother sat by and watched. Then my grandparents came over one day unexpectedly and took me away. I have seen my mom on occasion, but I haven't seen my father since that day."

"How did you get that scar?" Torch asks in a deadly, calm voice. He is talking about the half-an-inch-long scar on my forehead that I know is there because my mom told me it was a month or so after the cut healed.

"He threw an ice pack from a lunchbox at me. It cut me. My mom put Band-Aids on it. I wasn't worth the trip to the doctor's office," I quote his exact words.

"Did he…?" Torch asks, and I know exactly what he is asking.

"No, he didn't."

"Thank God." Torch lets out a sigh of relief, and I thank God above that nothing like that happened to me. Even though my situation isn't as bad as some people's, it has affected me my whole life.

"Come here, baby," Torch says before I am folded into his arms. I close my eyes. In his arms I feel like the whole world around me just melts away and everything will be okay. "I am so fucking sorry you had to suffer like that."

"It was a long time ago."

I feel him shake his head. "I know it was long ago, but that doesn't make it okay."

"I know," I say sadly.

"Go get ready. I gotta make some phone calls."

He slips out of bed and is out of the room a second later. I feel better telling him, that it is out in the open. I needed to get it off my chest. I had a sucky life growing up, but I won't allow that to dictate my life now.

Torch

Rage doesn't even come close to what I am feeling right now. *My* Kayla was treated like shit by her very own father.

I call Ryan. He is coming with a few brothers to get her deadbeat mom. Opening her home to her mother, who has done nothing but treat her like shit, shows what kind of person Kayla is. She is a hell of a lot more lenient than I am.

She is still upstairs getting ready when I hear four motorcycles pull up outside. Through our involvement with the MC, we all get paid from all the businesses we own. Kyle, Ryan, Trey, Techy, Me, and Butch are the originals. We started the MC from the ground up and have added members since then.

"What's up, man?" Techy asks when I walk outside to meet them.

"Kayla's mom called and is staying at Kayla's house for a while. Her dad may be a problem. He beat the shit out of her mom and was horrible to Kayla her whole life." I growl the last part as my anger flares again.

"He was mean to Kayla, how?"

All of the men in front of me are pissed off. "He liked to torture her because she's blind. He would purposely set things in her way, lock her in rooms, and neglect her." I clench my fists with the want to fucking kill the guy. I am controlling my anger as best I can only because of Kayla. I don't want her to get stressed while she's pregnant.

"Torch?" Kayla calls and I walk back into the house. I see her standing in tight-ass jeans, boots to her knees, and a mid-sleeve shirt that hugs her every curve as well as her tits. My dick stands at attention at the sight of those fuckers barely peeking out at the top of her shirt. Her hair is hanging down around her face and down her back. Her fuck-me lips are pouty and her eyes look like they are staring straight into your soul. She doesn't even know how gorgeous she is.

"You're a lucky fucker," Techy says behind me. I grin cockily, because that woman is mine.

I walk over to her and grab her hand. She immediately smiles that sweet-as-fuck smile. "You ready to go?" I ask. She nods and grabs her phone off the table she is standing next to.

She lets go of my hand and walks in front of me a few feet, her ass shaking in those jeans. I look over at Techy and the rest of the guys, who are looking at her ass, too. Taking my gun out of my back holster, I cock it and point it at them.

"Eyes off," I mouth and arch an eyebrow, ready to blow a fucking hole through them, brothers or not.

They all lift their hands up in the air in surrender and grin. I re-holster my gun, walk over to Kayla, and grab her ass. Mine.

"Come on, fuckers, let's go."

Kayla

When we hit the open road, I can't help but feel nervous. I am going home for the first time in over twenty years. That old fucking trailer holds too many bad memories. My father shouldn't be there. He's probably out getting high.

My mother would never leave him, just sat by and watched while I was treated like shit. I can't imagine how or why she would do that. The baby growing inside of me already means the world to me, and I would do anything to protect him.

I place my hand on my belly, rubbing. Wishing he were already here so I could hold him, love him. *Soon, baby boy.*

Torch puts his hand on top of mine, holding my belly with me. My heart squeezes at this man's gesture. God, I love him and wish I could have met him a long time ago. I hear the guys' motorcycles around Torch's truck as we go down the highway.

Two hours later, we pull to a stop and I know we are here. My stomach is in knots at the thought of being here after all these years, a place I thought I would never come back to.

"Fuck. This is where you lived?" Torch growls. I hear the steering wheel crunch as he tightens his hands on it.

"Let's go get this over with," I open my door, then hands reach inside and help me down. I know they're not Torch's, but one of the MC guy's, yet I'm not sure whose.

A hand wraps around mine. It's Torch this time. I let out a deep breath. He is here with me. Everything will be okay.

We walk toward the front door. I feel the presence of his brothers at my back, letting me know I have their support, which means more to me than they will ever know. Torch may not be their blood, but blood doesn't make you family.

I hear Torch knock and then the door creak open as it slides over the carpet from being broken.

"Kayla, I've missed you!" my mom says, and then her arms wrap around me. I don't hug her back. It feels wrong, so I push her gently away.

"I brought some people with me. This is my man. Those guys behind me are his friends."

"Why are they here? I thought you were getting dropped off," she says. My brow furrows in confusion. Why does she want me to get dropped off?

"Why did you think that?" I ask and feel the men at my back come closer. Torch puts an arm in front of me and pushes me slightly behind him.

"Well, I'll be damned. She will make me a pretty penny. Why didn't you tell me she is this good-looking?"

My hearts stops. My father is here. Did my mom try to set me up?

"Thanks for bringing her, man. I will take it from here."

"Motherfucker!" Torch roars, and I hear a loud noise, like something hitting the wall. My mother starts screaming, so I know Torch went after my father. One of the guys picks me up off the porch until we're standing in the yard.

"What kind of fucking father are you?" I hear Torch ask in a deadly voice that has chills running up my back. Then a gun cocks and my dad whimpers. "I should kill you now and do the world a favor, but that will be up to your daughter."

"Kayla," my mom begs. I feel her hands touch mine. I push them away, not wanting to touch a person like her. She tried to lure me here. Did she think Torch would just hand me over? He talked to her on the phone!

"Kayla, want me to kill him and get him out of your life forever?" My dad starts crying.

"Let's just fucking leave," I answer him. I hear another thump, then footsteps tell me Torch is walking off the porch and toward me.

"I had no choice, Kayla," my mom whispers, and my heart fractures a bit.

"Please, Mom, don't do this to me," I beg her. She lured me here so my dad could fucking sell me.

"Good-bye, Mom," I whisper to her before I turn around. When Torch leads me back to the truck, I hear her crying. My heart is breaking all over again. I want my mother to be there for me. I want her to be there when I have my baby, to love me, to tell me that everything will be okay, for her to be my mom. When I came here today, I was holding on to that hope, but my father has his hooks into her so deep she is brainwashed to the point she thinks this life is normal.

After Torch helps me into the truck, I lean my head against the back of the seat, closing my eyes in an effort to hold back the tears. I hear her screaming and it's killing me. I want to help her, but look what happened when I was going to. What else am I supposed to do?

Torch's door slams shut and he starts the truck, driving me away from this place. All ties have been broken now. My heart is hurting so bad from leaving my mom behind like that. Even though she has done shit for me, I'm devastated. She is still my mom. I rub my chest and rest my head against the window.

"Baby, come here," Torch says. I move over to the middle seat and move my head to his shoulder.

"I wanted to take her away from that life," I croak. I blink and a tear falls down my cheek.

"I know, baby. We all did. But your mom can't be helped until she wants to be." He kisses the top of my head. I wrap my arm around his, hugging it.

"I just wanted a mom. I want my mom to be there when I have my baby, someone I can call in the middle of the night when he's sick and I don't know what to do." I sniff as tears are rolling down my face steadily now.

"I feel betrayed in the worst way. I came here today with a small glimmer of hope that she could be that person, but she was luring me in so my father could sell me or some fucked-up shit." I wipe my eyes and close them, feeling exhausted all of a sudden.

"Sleep, baby," Torch whispers and I nod.

Torch

Furious isn't a word I'd use to describe how I feel right now. I wanted to kill her dad, because what kind of fucking father plans on selling his own kid? Kayla was so fucking strong and held her head up.

Her crying is breaking my fucking heart. Seeing her so fucking sad today is messing with me, and I don't like it. I know in this moment I will do everything in my power to make sure she doesn't hurt like this again.

I pull over to the side of the road and open my truck door. I lay Kayla down onto the seat gently before I silently shut the door and walk a few feet with my hands behind my head. I need to get ahold of myself before I turn my ass back around and kill her dad.

"You have fucking more restraint than I do," Butch says. I look behind me to see all my brothers standing there.

"I want to kill that bastard, but I needed to get Kayla out of that fucked-up situation."

"How is she?" Butch asks. I look around at him, surprised. Butch usually doesn't ask questions like this. He is looking through the driver's side window at Kayla.

"She fell asleep. I am going to stop at a steakhouse in town for dinner. You guys are welcome," I tell them and they nod.

I climb back into the truck, putting Kayla's head in my lap so she can sleep comfortably. I sound like a fucking pussy, but I don't care. I care about this woman, and I'm not ashamed to admit it.

For the next two hours, the drive back to Raleigh is silent aside from Kayla's breathing. I put my hand on her still flat stomach, convinced I'm going to have a son this time.

Kayla

"Baby, time to wake up."

"Hmm." I move my head and bury it deeper into my pillow.

"Time to eat."

At that I sit straight up and get dizzy. "Whoa," I mumble and hold my head.

"You okay?" Torch asks.

Yawning, I pull my hair up in a bun at the top of my head. "Yeah I just sat up too quickly."

He doesn't say anything, but gets out of the truck. I open my door and wait for him to help me down.

"How are you feeling, Kayla?" Ryan asks. I smile. "I'm okay."

Torch wraps his arm around my waist and we walk into wherever we are eating. The door opens, and I'm hit with the smell of steak. My mouth starts watering and my stomach growls loudly. The men behind me laugh.

"My baby is hungry," Torch says and rubs my stomach. "Starving," I tell him. The waitress seats us.

"Torch, where are you?" I call as I walk down the stairs later that night. His arms wrap around me, and I lay my head on his warm chest.

"Why are you out of bed?" he asks. I roll my eyes. He all of a sudden thinks I am super fragile just because of everything that happened today. Yeah, today was freaking awful, but I feel relieved because all ties to my old life are now over and done with.

I run my hands up and down his back then let them dip down inside the back of his pants a bit.

Should I? I think to myself.

I grab the ends of his underwear in the back gently so he won't know what I am about to do. Biting my lip, I try to stop myself from laughing. I tend to do that when I am trying to be sneaky about doing something.

With a tight grip I pull his underwear up, giving him a major wedgie.

"Kayla!" he yells and lets me go. I hear a bar stool fall onto the ground and I lie down on the floor, laughing and just imagining the look on his face right now.

"You'll pay for that," he warns, and I hear his thundering steps. Scrambling to my feet, I run out of the kitchen and hide behind one of the couches. If I didn't know this house so well, I wouldn't be able to do this.

I put my hand over my mouth trying to stop my giggling. *Just shut up, Kayla. You just started a war.*

"Kayla, where did you go? Come out, come out wherever you are," he sings, and it's fucking hilarious coming from a man like him.

"Dude, what the fuck are you doing?" Techy asks, and I burst out laughing. When did he get here? Oh my god, I wish I could see Torch's face right now. I lie down on the ground again, holding my stomach.

Torch plucks me off the ground and sets me in his lap on the couch. I wipe my eyes and start laughing again.

"What the fuck did she do?" Techy asks. Between laughs I tell him about giving Torch a wedgie. I don't care if it makes me look childish or not.

"Oh shit, man." Techy starts laughing, and I feel Torch vibrating with his own laughter even though he is trying to hide it.

"Why are you here, man?" Torch asks Techy. I smack his chest. *Rude much?*

"Babe, I was just asking the man." He knows why I hit him.

"My TV broke and the game is on," Techy explains. The TV comes on a moment later. I lean back against Torch until my eyes start to drop and I fall asleep.

"On your knees." I do as I am told and get down on my hands and knees, exposing my backside to Torch. His hand runs over my butt cheeks and my pussy. I move my hips back, wanting more.

"Patience," he scolds and smacks my backside. I jump in shock and moan at the heady pain, and then get turned on even more.

"Do you want to come, baby?" Torch asks. I nod my head frantically. He has been touching me for the last hour, getting me riled up. I guess he is punishing me for the damn wedgie.

"Please," I beg, needing the ache to disappear, needing to be filled with the intense pleasure Torch gives me.

"You never beg for me."

Before I can say anything, his mouth is wrapped around my clit and I scream as my orgasm crashes through me like a tsunami. My legs are shaking uncontrollably; my arms give out and I fall onto my face, the rest of my body falling to the side.

Once I catch my breath, Torch taps my butt to get my attention. "Back on your knees." On shaking limbs, I do as I'm told. I feel his dick at my entrance and push back until he is completely inside me, filling me to the hilt.

His fist tightens around my hair and pushes me down, so my face is on the mattress, my back arched. He pulls out and slams back in, pulling my hair with the movement. I scream at the pain and the pleasure.

He slams in harder and harder, and I find myself pushing back against him. I moan loudly. The pleasure is beyond intense. I love every minute of it.

He pounds into me harder and quicker until my breath almost stills. I'm straining, reaching for that orgasm that is thundering toward me. My legs are trembling again as I grab the sheets, bracing myself. My toes are curled under.

His thumb rubs my clit and my body shoots up off the bed. I grab the headboard as I scream, my body moving all over, and I feel my pussy milking his cock and hear him roar when his load fills me.

I let out a deep breath, exhausted, and fall to the side yet again. He wraps his arms around me, our limbs entwined.

ten

Kayla

"Girls' day!" Jean screams as she runs into the house. I hear the door hit the wall. I smile and stand up. She wraps her arms around me. We are going to get a mani-pedis and a haircut. Since I can't paint my own nails and toes, I need this every few weeks.

"Be careful with my girl. It's all on me. A prospect will be tailing you as usual," Torch tells Jean and then his lips are on my forehead. "Have fun, baby."

"I will. See you later." I kiss his cheek. Jean wraps her arm around mine and leads me out of the house.

She opens her car door and helps me inside. It's weird getting in a car since I've been used to Torch's truck.

She gets in the driver's side, and then we're gone. She turns on the radio and starts singing along at the top of her lungs. There is something infectious about this woman. She is so happy-go-lucky she could make the meanest and unhappiest person smile.

"I so need to get my nails done! It's been forever. I need good dick hands."

I burst out laughing at her. Dick hands?

"What? While I'm sucking his dick I need pretty hands while I pump that bitch."

I lay against the window laughing. I didn't expect her to say that, so that makes it a million times funnier.

"Bell is at her mother's for the day, so she couldn't come. Chrystal is at the center running things, so it's just you and me."

She talks the whole way to the salon, answering herself most of the time. I'm fine with that, because I zone out while I hear the prospect on his motorcycle driving behind us. Torch insisted I wear my cut today. I guess it's his way of protecting me even when he isn't around.

We pull up in front of the salon, and Jean walks us inside. They seat us for our pedicures within minutes. Once they get started on my feet, I ask Jean. "How did you and…?"

"Jack," she answers for me.

"How did you guys meet?" I lean back in my seat and close my eyes, enjoying this.

"I was working at a gas station outside of town. One day he came in and said I was his. I didn't know the guy from shit, but I looked at him and knew, just knew I was going to love this man. So I did what any woman would do. I quit my job then and there and sat astride his motorcycle. I haven't left his side since."

"Wow!"

"You have a similar story with Torch, though, he kidnapped you." Jean laughs. I hear someone run into something. They must have heard that part.

"Don't fall, sugar. He didn't *literally* kidnap her," Jean clarifies. I can just imagine her smirk.

I know now the MC life isn't for everyone, but the women who can accept it will be happy and lucky women. Torch is the greatest man I have ever met. I feel so protected, like nothing can hurt me when he's around. I crave that safety.

I know he's it for me, have known it for a while. I mean, who wouldn't fall for that man? He is a total badass, and I have witnessed that. He is dangerous, but I know he would do anything to protect the ones he cares for. He is an alpha male through and through, but he also has that gooey center I love.

"I'm pregnant."

"What!" I screech.

Jean laughs. "I'm pregnant. Well, just barely. I am just a couple of weeks."

"Congratulations, girl!" I am so excited for her. My baby will have someone to grow up with. "Have you told Jack yet?"

"Not yet. Well, I may have left the pregnancy test on his motorcycle with a note on it. So we may be getting a visit later."

I nod knowing she will definitely be getting a visit.

Two hours later, I am getting my hair done. My nails and toes are all prettied up. That's when I hear the door to the salon open and motorcycle boots hit the tiled flooring.

"Jean!"

Yep, he's here. I smother my smile with my hand.

"Yes, Jackson?" she sings.

"Is this what I think it is?"

"Yeah. I'm pregnant," she confirms, and I hear him running then kissing her. "Thank you for making me the happiest man alive."

Here come the water works. Damn pregnancy hormones. I hear him telling her he loves her and am sobbing by that point.

"What's wrong with you, Kayla?" Jean laughs.

I wipe my eyes and laugh. "Pregnancy hormones. I cry at the drop of a hat. Congratulations, you guys." I smile and sit back in my seat to let the lady trim my hair and layer it again.

An hour later, Jean drops me off and helps me into the house. When I walk in, something wet touches my hand. I pull away before reaching my hand back down. Fur! I rub my hand down a hairy back. A dog!

"You like him?" Torch asks.

My eyes widen and my mouth falls open a bit. "You got me a dog?"

"A protection dog."

I bend down and hug the dog. *I always wanted a dog!* "What kind is he? Or is it a girl?"

"He's a German Shepherd," Torch answers. I sit down on my butt. The dog crawls into my lap, and I laugh because he is huge. I fall back a bit when he licks my face.

"Thank you!" I gently push the dog off of my lap and stand up. Torch pulls me over into his arms and kisses me on the mouth.

"Anything for you, babe."

I almost melt into a pile of goo. This man is too much.
"What's his name?"
"Mika."
"Come on, I think you need to be rewarded." I grab his shirt and pull him up the stairs with me.

Walking into the bedroom, I shut the door behind us. I sink down to my knees on the floor in front of Torch, grab his belt buckle, and unbuckle it. I unbutton his pants and pull down the zipper then sneak my hands inside and pull out his dick.

"Stop, baby." His hands stop mine.

"What?" I ask, my mouth only inches from his tip.

He lifts me off my knees and up to my feet. "You never get on your knees for anyone," he growls and presses his mouth to mine. "You are to be worshiped,"—his lips trail down to my throat then down to my breasts—"cherished"—his lips trail down to my belly button—"You are my Queen and will be treated as such." He presses his lips to my belly one last time before he pushes me down onto the bed.

I'm in shock from his words. My heart soars and butterflies swarm my belly. I smile at how amazing this man is.

"Whatever did I do to deserve someone like you?" I whisper and touch his cheek.

"Baby, I am the luckiest man alive." He kisses me, and I wrap my leg around his waist. He is completely naked.

His hips lean forward until his dick is at my entrance. I raise my hips, taking him inside me a bit. I moan at the heat radiating off of him and clench my walls. He hisses and pushes all the way to the hilt.

I throw my head back and drag my nails down his back. His lips drag lazily down my neck. Then he pulls back and pushes slowly back inside. He does this over and over with leisurely strokes that are driving me wild.

"More," I demand and gasp when he hits that spot inside of me.

"No, let me love you."

In this moment, I want nothing more than to see this man above me. I want to look into his eyes and see what he is feeling right now, see him.

The next thirty minutes are filled with me quivering as the need gets bigger and bigger. The burn is slow, but gets hotter and hotter to the point where I'm holding back a scream and am straining, reaching for more.

He pulls back to the tip and pushes back in, but this time he pinches my clit. I scream. "Ahh!" I grab at the sheets trying to hold myself and stop me from shooting off the bed. Torch roars his release and falls to my side, our limbs tangled together.

We lie in silence trying to catch our breath. "Go get ready. I'm taking you out tonight." He smacks my bare ass cheek. I laugh at him.

"Yes, sir," I salute then crawl to the side of the bed. Torch isn't a fancy restaurant person, and neither am I.

I go into the bathroom and hop into the shower. Only moments later, I hear the glass door open and know Torch is standing on the other end of the shower. We don't wash each other, because we won't be leaving for a long time if we do.

I step out and wrap a towel around my waist then grab the hair dryer out of the cabinet and get busy drying my hair. I don't wear makeup, so it's super easy for me to get ready.

After my hair is dry, I go to my closet and put on a pair of shorts and a flowy t-shirt that hangs off one shoulder. I have on a strapless bra. Last, I put on a pair of sandals.

"Ready!" I call to Torch.

"Okay." His voice is right next to my ear. I scream and hold my chest as my heart almost pops out of it. "You scared the shit out of me."

"Sorry," he murmurs and kisses my forehead.

"I fed the dog and took him out. I have a backyard that is fenced in, so you can let him in and out yourself without worrying about him running away. Which he shouldn't, because he's your dog."

"Thank you, but come on, let's go. I am starving!" I smack him on the butt and smile at him. His teeth bite at my bottom lip and pull.

"Hmmm, feeling frisky?" I tease and lick my bottom lip.

"We better go or we won't make it out that door," he growls and kisses me on the lips.

"No, I'm starving." He pulls away and grabs my hand. I follow behind him down the stairs. We stop on the porch while he locks the door, then he takes my hand again and we walk down the steps.

I smell the night air and smile. I love being out in the country like this. I feel incredibly happy right now.

I hear the truck door open and then I am lifted off my feet as he sets me inside. I attempted to climb inside by myself once, but I almost killed myself. It's really high up, and I can't see anything.

He buckles me in and kisses me on the lips before shutting the door. I touch my mouth and smile. This man makes me feel like a teenager at times I get so freaking giddy.

He slams his door, and then we are off. I roll down my window and set my feet on the dashboard, close my eyes and let the night wind flow through my hair. He turns on the radio, then grabs my hand and kisses the back of it.

"I don't know what I would do without you," I voice.

"Same with you, baby. You aren't ever getting rid of me," he promises me and lays our joined hands on the seat between us.

"Really? What if I ran away?" I tease.

"I'd kidnap your ass again."

I laugh at that and shake my head, then turn it back toward the window.

We park outside of the restaurant. I sit up in my seat and hear Torch shut his door before mine pops open a minute later. His hands wrap around my waist and lift me down onto the ground.

"How many?" the waitress asks.

"Just two," he answers her.

"Follow me."

We do and sit down in the booth, Torch sitting directly beside me. He grabs my hands and sets them in his lap. I lay my head on his shoulder for a second before sitting back up.

"Here are your menus, and if you need anything else, let me know." the waitress says in her overly cheerful voice.

Torch spends the next few minutes going over the menu with me. I get the steak with mozzarella cheese on top and shrimp.

The waitress comes back and takes our order. Torch orders for himself and me.

"This is basically our first date," I tell him and shift in my seat.

"I know. I just now fucking realized it."

"It's okay." I smile and rub my thumb across the top of his hand.

"If you had asked me a couple months ago if this would be my life, I would have said heck no. I didn't live. I lived in my own little world. I wouldn't miss my time with you for anything in this world."

He kisses my forehead. I grin. This is Torch's way of being emotional.

"Paisley and the MC were my life. I hadn't been with a woman in a long time before you. I didn't want my baby girl to meet any woman in my life until I was sure I wanted to be with her. My life in the MC is different, and it's not for everyone. It's dangerous at times, but we diffuse that because we protect our women above everything else. It takes a special breed of woman to accept that lifestyle. The thing with men like us is, when we have an ole lady, for us it's the same thing as marriage of sorts. The guys, my brothers, will do whatever to protect you like I would."

"I know. I like your own special breed. There isn't one thing I would change about you." I rise up and kiss his cheek, then rest my forehead there for a few seconds before sitting back in my seat and put my hand on my stomach.

"Here are your rolls." The waitress pops back over and I hear the sound of a plate hitting the tabletop. The smell of the rolls hits me, and I move my hand forward slowly. It hits the glass, so I retract my hand and move it over until the tips of my fingers touch the rolls.

Grasping one, I tear a piece off and pop it into my mouth. I groan. Holy shit, this is amazing.

"Here is some cinnamon butter." Torch touches the bottom on the side of my hand.

I tear off another piece and dip it in the butter, then take a bite and roll my eyes back in my head. I'm in heaven. I could eat these and be full.

"I'm taking some of these home," I tell Torch.

He laughs at me and kisses me on the cheek. I probably look like a slob right now, but I don't care. I know some girls are ashamed to eat in front of people, which I totally get. You don't want people to think you are a fat ass and be like 'Why is she eating that when she is fat?' I got over that when I realized people are going to judge no matter what I do.

"I'm not sure I want to do that. If a roll makes you look like that, I need to step up my game," he jokes and runs his hand over the crotch of my shorts.

"Baby, if I come any harder with you, I'll stay passed out."

"I-I-I…your food," the waitress says and sets our food down. I hear her running off in the other direction.

"Oops," I tell Torch, and he bursts out laughing. Hey, it's not my fault I didn't see her there. Pun intended.

"Here is your food." Torch grabs my hand and touches it to the side of my plate. He grabs my other hand and has it touch my fork and knife.

"Thank you." I grab my utensils and get busy cutting up my steak.

Torch

I shake from laughter even as I tell Kayla where everything is so she can eat. I know she could do it alone, but I want to help her.

She was telling me if she came any harder she would pass out, and she said it at the exact moment the waitress came over with our food. Her face turned a million different shades of red, then she set the food down and ran off.

I can't help but fucking notice how beautiful Kayla is tonight. I am one lucky fucker, but on the other hand I am not. Too many fuckers stare at her, and it's taking everything in me not to grab my fork and gouge out some eyes.

What makes her more beautiful to me is how she accepts all of me. The MC life. Everything. Her carrying my baby in her stomach. How her eyes light as she smiles that smile that makes my heart hurt.

I sound like a pussy, but I know in this moment that I love this woman. I believe I did the moment I met her. When she looked up at me without seeing me, scared out of her mind, and still she clung to me. Possessiveness overrode everything else.

Kayla fills that void inside of me that I never knew was there. The need to protect her is overpowering. I can't stand anyone looking at her with want, because she is mine and I'm not sure how I would do without this woman in my life. She is mine, and I will kill any fucker that tries to take her away from me.

eleven

Kayla

A week later

I moan as I puke again into the toilet. Morning sickness isn't fun at all.

Torch sets a cold washcloth on my neck. I should be embarrassed puking in front of him, but I'm not. He knocked me up, so he shall suffer, too.

"Dude, I need something for my stomach." I shudder and hold my middle, feeling weak. I've had low blood sugar for as long as I can remember, but it gets worse and better in spells. This is taking a toll on it as I puke every morning and sometimes after I eat something my stomach doesn't agree with.

"I need to eat before my sugar gets too low. I haven't had a problem with it in almost a year, but I am feeling the signs. Shaky hands, light-headedness," I tell Torch and stand up. I sway to the side. He catches me and lifts me off the ground.

"Let me brush my teeth really quick." I grab my toothbrush and scrub my teeth. Torch keeps a strong hand on my waist, making sure I don't fall.

"Let me check your sugar, babe," he says and lays me down on the bed.

He puts the needle in the poker then wipes my finger with an alcohol swab, then presses the poker to my finger and clicks the button. I flinch at the needle, but hold still. He squeezes my finger until a drop of blood sits at the top, then puts the strip in the meter and drips the blood. It beeps when it has enough blood.

Your blood glucose is forty-five

No wonder I feel like shit.

"Babe, can you grab me some juice?" I don't feel like getting up.

"Yeah, lie here." I hear him run out of the room. I wipe my forehead with the back of my hand.

When I hear him walking back up the stairs, I sit up in bed. He sets the drink in my hand and I chug it down. "Here is some chocolate." He puts it in my hand next. Is it bad I want to cry and laugh at the same time? Dang pregnancy hormones.

"Babe, it's just chocolate," he says in amusement. He must have seen my tearful expression.

"I'm pregnant. I can be emotional if I want to." I pucker my bottom lip before taking a bite.

"You're too fucking cute," he says and picks me up off the bed. I swing my legs while he is carrying me down the stairs, eating my chocolate.

He sits down on the couch with me in his lap, and I snuggle up to him. He grabs the throw blanket off the back of the couch and I tuck it under my neck, the chocolate forgotten and on the table in front of the couch.

"Tell me about your childhood," I ask him and entwine our fingers.

"I was raised by Mom and Dad. They were good parents, but when I got Paisley's mom pregnant, my dad kicked me out because I disgraced the family. I moved out and busted my ass to provide for Paisley's mom and me.

"She had the baby. I was so in love with my little girl. Paisley's mom didn't like that and didn't want a kid to tie her down and take all the attention away from her. She left in the middle of the night leaving only a note telling us good-bye.

"I was mad, because Paisley wouldn't have her mom, and I wanted that for her. A few years went by until I got the papers ready for her to sign her rights over for good. She did that, and that was the last time I saw her."

"I haven't seen my parents since the day they kicked me out. My father wanted me to become a big shot lawyer just like him, but I wasn't made for that. My mother was crying. I know she didn't want me to go, but she didn't stop him from kicking me out either."

"I raised my baby girl by myself for years, had her in daycare, hired babysitters. I saved everything I could, but my baby girl never went without and lived well. When I met Kyle, Ryan, Butch, Trey, and Techy, we put our money together and opened some businesses. We now own forty."

"I'm so sorry about your parents and Paisley's mom. I don't know how a parent could do such a thing." I shake my head in disbelief and grab the bottom of his shirt, twisting it in my hands.

"Me either, baby," he agrees and kisses my temple. I smile as butterflies swarm through my stomach.

"Marry me," he says out of the blue.

I gasp in shock. Did he just say what I think he did?

"What?" I say, shocked. I sit up in his lap.

"Marry me, baby," he repeats, and I gape.

I love this man, but I don't want to be married to him if he doesn't love me. I can't and won't. But I also can't bear the thought of not being with him. "I won't get married unless I know the guy I'm with loves me." This will either end well or badly. I do believe deep in my heart that he does love me.

"Who says I don't?"

"Do you?" I ask, my voice small and my anxiety off the charts.

"I do, baby, more than life itself. I haven't voiced that shit, but I do. I think I did from the moment you clung to me after your almost kidnapping."

My mouth hits the floor. I can't believe what he just told me. A tear escapes and I let out a sob. I place my hands over my face and cry, because I never thought this would ever happen.

"Baby, shh." Torch pulls my hand from my face. I bury my face in the crook of his neck. His strong arms wrap around me, holding me to him.

"I love you, too," I whisper to him.

"You do?" I can hear the smile in his voice.

Lifting my head up, I smile. "Of course I do, silly man."

"Well, let's go get married then," he says and stands us up and runs up the stairs. I laugh at his silly antics.

"Get dressed, babe. I am not waiting another second to get married. Calling the courthouse. We can have a big wedding later." He sets me down on my feet.

"What about wedding rings?" I ask before he walks out of the room.

"I already have them."

"What?"

He chuckles at me. "Baby, I was planning on doing this for a while." He smacks my ass. "Now, go get ready."

Once I'm dressed, I walk out of the bedroom. Torch plucks me off my feet and walk-runs down the stairs. I laugh at this man and smile, because my heart is heavy with joy he placed there. My husband.

I am married. I am married to Torch. I am Mrs. Daniels. Now we are heading back to his house. We're going on our honeymoon later after we have a big wedding in front of our friends.

Torch plucks me out of the truck, and we walk up the steps at the front of the house. Once we reach the door, I am swept off my feet bridal style. "Welcome home, Mrs. Daniels."

He pushes the door open and slams it shut behind him then walks slowly up the stairs to our bedroom.

My back touches the bed as he lays me gently down. Torch kisses me while I run my hands down his arms. His hand cups my jaw, stroking my cheekbone.

He pulls back and unbuttons my shirt, then rises up and I follow. His breath is mixing with mine, and I know he is staring into my eyes.

I raise my arms above my head and he slips off my tank top, then my bra joins it on the floor. He unbuttons my shorts and pulls them down my legs with my panties.

Reaching for him, I grab the button of his shirt. I climb up on my knees and pull his shirt over his head then run my hands down his chest, abs, and sides. Touch is everything to me since I can't see.

I unbutton his pants. He takes over taking them off, and I hear them hit the floor. He's completely naked in front of me right now. Just like me.

"Let me touch you. I can't see you, but I can feel you," I whisper as I run my hand up his belly to his chest then his face. My fingers move over his full lips, his strong jaw line, the stubble on his cheeks. I touch his nose. It has a small scar in the middle. I drag my hands up to his hair. It's cut closer to his head on the sides and longer at the top.

I run my hands down his back, using my nails. His back is strong, his shoulders large. I touch his butt cheeks. They are two hard globes. I grab both of them in my hands and squeeze, and laugh when he jumps.

His mouth slams down onto mine, stopping my laughter. He gently pushes me against the bed. I wrap my legs around his waist, wanting him as close to me as humanly possible. He pulls away from my mouth and moves down my body.

His tongue laps at my folds, and I shudder at the pure pleasure he is bringing me. Once he reaches my clit, I moan deeply. His tongue moves up and down, bringing me closer and closer to my peak.

His mouth moves down until his tongue enters my pussy. I open my legs wider and move my hips, trying to pull him deeper. He moans and it vibrates his tongue. I cry out and grab the back of his head.

He moves his head back up to my clit, then two fingers enter me. Those two fingers are hitting that special spot while he sucks my clit deep into his mouth and moans. I cross the finish line and throw my head back, moaning loudly as spasms rock me.

His body moves up mine until his dick is at my entrance, where he slowly enters me until he is sheathed to the hilt. But he doesn't move.

"I love you, baby. I should have said it sooner. I love everything about you." He kisses me gently, tenderly, then moves inside of me while kissing me. His movements are gentle, tender, and loving. This is making love.

Tears come to my eyes at the immense love I feel for this man. I cry as he kisses me and loves me in a way I have never felt before and want to always feel.

We come at the same time.

This sealing our forevers together.

Torch

I look down at Kayla after we just made love. I didn't think I could love anyone like this, but I love her with everything in me. I never realized how much until this very moment. She brings me peace.

Today is the first day of the rest of our lives. Together. I would do anything for her, love her unconditionally. I may be turning soft, but I am only soft for this woman right here and only when I'm with her. With everyone else, I'm still Torch. Torch, who favors a torch during an interrogation.

Kayla will be the only person who sees my vulnerable side. The only one I will be with like this. She may have not been my first, but she sure as fuck will be my last.

To my forever with my Kayla.

twelve

Waking up after a night filled with sex, I turn over and lay my head on Torch's chest. His breathing is deep and steady. With my hand over his heart I feel his heartbeat.

"Good morning, Mrs. Daniels."

I grin from ear-to-ear at hearing him calling me Mrs. Daniels. I will never ever tire of him calling me that.

"Good morning, Husband." I rise up and kiss him. The kiss lands at the corner of his mouth as his hand fists into my hair.

"Want to go out for breakfast?" I ask. He yawns and turns over, taking me with him, his face nuzzling the side of my neck. "I am going to have my breakfast now." He bites my earlobe.

"Oh yeah?" I tilt my head. He takes advantage, biting the side of my neck. His lips trail down my chest until they reach my breasts. He pops the nipple into his mouth then lets it go with a pop. I moan as the pleasure shoots down to my pussy, soaking me instantly.

Torch touches my dripping folds and moves to the other breast, showing it just as much attention.

His mouth moves down to my stomach and presses a kiss to my belly button. Then he is there. I place my legs on either side of his shoulders as he works me over. It doesn't take long before I come.

While I'm still coming down, he crawls up my body and enters me with one thrust. I know in this moment this won't be like the sweet love-making from last night. No, this is hot, claiming sex.

He hammers inside of me and spreads my legs open wide, so he can thrust deeper. I bite my lip and moan, grab the sheets beside me and hold on for dear life; because this man knows the true meaning of fucking.

After we are finished, he falls onto the bed beside me and places his hand on my stomach, which is starting to show a small baby bump. He gently runs his hand over it again and again.

"I can't believe I'm going to be a mom." The realization is sinking in.

Torch moves and then his lips are on my stomach. I smile and put my hand on the back of his head, running my hands through his short hair.

"Hi, my son. I can't wait to meet you, buy you your first motorcycle, teach you how to be a man, those first steps." He kisses my belly and lays his head on top of it like he is trying to listen for the baby.

If it's possible, I just fell more in love with this man. He couldn't get any more amazing.

"Let's get my babies fed." Torch gets out of bed first, then he plucks me out butt naked, carries me down the stairs, and deposits me on top of the barstool.

"What are you craving this morning?"

"French toast?" I say, hopeful.

"You got it." He kisses me and walks away. I touch my tingling lips. I can't believe my life now. It went from being alone and thinking I was going to be that way for a while to being married and pregnant.

I wouldn't change a damn thing.
"Hey, Torch," I call
"Yeah?"
"I love you." I smile and hear him walking over to me.
"I love you, too, baby. Forever and always."

thirteen

Torch

"Ryan and Butch, I need you to keep an eye on the guys who weren't around when we bombed those fuckers. Most of them are gone, but a small few are still hanging around." Kyle looks directly at Butch and Ryan, who nod their heads in confirmation.

"I have some guys coming today to install bulletproof glass in the slots in front of your guys' gates and surrounding your house. What happened here is inexcusable, and the safety of yourself and your family is important. This won't happen again."

I nod my head, agreeing with Kyle one hundred percent. I want Kayla to be as safe as possible, especially at our home. She should be able to go outside and be completely safe. The gate in front of our house is unbreakable, and the wall surrounding us is impervious; and if someone tries, I am immediately alerted by an alarm and so are all the guys in the club. Someone climbing the gate around our house is up to no good.

All of our businesses are legit, but we have people try to move in and take our businesses by making threats and breaking and entering. It's happening less and less, but we won't take any chances.

"I believe a congrats is in order. Torch, I see you and Kayla got married over the weekend." I smirk at Kyle, who is doing the same to me. I told him just two years ago that I would never get married.

"Congrats, man," Ryan says and smacks me on the back.

"Thanks, I needed to tie her ass to me, so now she can't leave," I joke and the other guys join along. Though, I'm not really joking. Kayla is mine.

Kyle continues the church meeting. "We have a woman here with her eighteen-month-old daughter who needs protection. Since this isn't an easy case to take on, I'm going to bring her in so she can tell her story." We all nod.

He walks out of the room, and a minute later a toddler walks into the room carrying a blanket tucked under her neck. The little girl looks over at Ryan. I watch him stiffen and my eyes widen as she raises her little arms while heading over to him. He picks her up and she lays her head down on his shoulder.

"I can take her," the mother says, and I watch as Ryan looks up at her. His whole entire body jerks. I look at the mother. I can see why he is reacting this way; she is exactly his type, which is innocent and sweet.

"You can sit here," Butch says and stands up. She sits down beside Ryan, who is still staring directly at her.

"Myra, explain everything," Kyle bluntly orders her.

She lets out a deep breath and runs a hand down her face. Dark circles under her eyes tell us she is exhausted. "I am a doctor. I was coming home from the clinic. A babysitter was watching Mia. When I walked into my house, I saw the babysitter on her knees in front of a man who was holding a gun to her head. My baby was sitting right beside her. They didn't notice me, so I reached inside of my purse and grabbed the gun I always carry with me."

She looks over at her daughter for a split second before continuing. "I already had my gun out and the safety off when my purse scraped the wall. Then the man saw me and pointed the gun at my daughter, then at me. I pulled the trigger, no hesitation.

"The police came. The guy lived, but what I didn't know was that he was the son of the man that led the Satan's Rejects in my town. My babysitter owed him money and he was coming to collect. I have been getting threats in the form of letters and voicemails. The police can't protect me. I live just in the next town over."

Kyle stares at her and I do the same. "We will provide protection in exchange for your services."

Her eyes widen like she can't believe it. "Anything. I just want my daughter safe." Kyle nods, and before he can say anything else, Ryan asks, "Where's your man?"

I grin, because that fucker is hooked already or he wouldn't be asking. All of the brothers in the room grin. "He's on drugs. It's really bad. I had him sign his rights over, so he is out of the picture." She smiles at him, and I see Ryan jolt in his seat again.

"I need to put you in one of the safe houses instead of the center, because you have a job."

"No. She stays with me," Ryan says sternly. This time I chuckle.

"What?" she gapes at him.

"My house has top notch security, plus I can protect you and Mia."

He's got her now. He included the little girl.

"If you're sure..." she trails off. I sit back with my hands behind my head, looking at Kyle, who is grinning.

"Bite."

I look back at Mia, who is now sitting up as she says, "Bite" again.

"You need anything else, boss?" Ryan asks Kyle.

"We covered everything."

Without saying anything else, Ryan stands up with the little girl while she is tugging on his dog tags. "Let's go get her fed."

Myra stares up at him, looking shocked before she can cover it up. She grabs her diaper bag and purse and follows him out of the room, shutting the door behind them.

"He's fucked," Butch says and we all laugh.

"About time," Kyle agrees and chuckles along with us.

Kayla

What the fuck is all the noise? I am sitting on the couch eating chocolate, while my dog is sitting beside me. Once Torch leaves, Mika stays glued to my side. I enjoy the company.

Grabbing my phone, I dial Torch's number. "Hey, baby. I'm heading outside now. I hear the alarm!"

"Torch, why is it going off right now? I was sitting on the couch and it keeps going off like crazy for no reason."

"Kayla, go upstairs into our bedroom, then hide in the panic room inside of the closet. Take Mika with you. Someone is trying to get over the gate and wall."

Panic overcomes me. I jump off the couch. "Mika, come." I run toward the stairs. Mika comes up beside me, his body brushing my legs. I hurry up the stairs and into our bedroom, rush into the closet, where I get on my hands and knees, crawling until I reach the hidden keypad on the wall. I climb inside as soon as the door opens, Mika climbing in, too. Then I shut the door and lock it.

"I'm inside," I whisper. I can hear my heart pounding in my chest so loudly I'm afraid the intruders might hear.

Then I hear gunshots outside, and I know it's not Torch.

"They're shooting, Torch," I whisper again and close my eyes, afraid.

"We're almost there, baby."

I let out a deep breath.

The minutes that pass by are agony. I hear noises as someone is trying to break through the gate. I can hear the metal.

That's when I hear the sound of motorcycles. A *lot* of them. Then silence.

The wait is excruciating.

"Baby, it's safe, you can come out."

I almost collapse onto the ground with relief, but instead I unlock the door and step out into the closet.

Torch

Once the alarm hits our phones, all of the brothers run outside and hop on their bikes, no questions asked. I stay on the phone with her the whole time, listening to the fear in her voice. I don't think they can get into the house, because they would have to use bombs to get through; and the top of the wall has electricity, so the chances of them getting across is nonexistent.

When we pull up in front of my house, we see two fucking teenagers with guns in their hands standing at the gate. They look at us and their eyes widen like deer caught in headlights. We pull over, and I climb off my motorcycle pissed the fuck off. Who are they, shooting around my house? Kayla could have been outside.

I walk straight up to their faces and pluck the guns from their hands, handing them over to Butch, who walked up beside me.

"Why?!" I yell into their faces. They cringe and look away. "Are you shooting at my gate?"

They shake and their faces pale with fear. I grab the one on the right by the front of his shirt. "Don't make me ask again," I say lowly, with pure menace.

"I was paid one hundred dollars to shoot at your gate," he stutters, sweat dripping down his temple and the side of his face. I throw him away from me, disgusted.

"Who put you up to this?" I ask them as I take my gun out, running my hands along it.

"I can't tell you. Th-they w-will kill me," the one on the left says as he backs away only to bump into another brother.

"Don't make me ask again." I click the safety off. They gulp and raise their hands up in front of them.

"The Satan's Rejects," the one on the right whispers. My whole body stiffens with pure rage. Those fuckers need to be taken the fuck out.

I turn around and look at Kyle. He is pissed and nods his head. They will suffer. Kyle steps forward and gets into the kids' faces. "This is war. Tell them that. They messed with the wrong fucking club."

They nod so hard I wouldn't be surprised if they broke something. Then they run away from us and into the woods.

"War is happening, guys, but what they don't know is we are trained. Those guys are kids on the street, playing gangster. We already took half of them out. The other clubs wouldn't dare mess with us. The next city over harbors their leftover members. This will make a statement; they wouldn't dare face the consequences. They are motherfucking trafficking girls. That is something we cannot let stand. It's time to tell the others."

'The others' are our MC buddies throughout the state. They won't tolerate this either.

"Prospects are at your guys' disposal for watching out for your women."

Taking my phone out, I call Kayla. "Baby, it's safe. You can come out."

I hear her sigh of relief and unlock my gate. A few seconds later, I see the front door open and she steps out with Mika by her side.

"Torch!" she calls and I walk up the yard to her.

"I'm here." I pull her into my arms and press her cheek against my chest. I kiss the top of her head and let out a shaky breath. Imagining something happening to her is scary, and I can't bear to think of it. I love this woman with everything in me. My wife.

fourteen

Kayla

Later that day.

"I love you, husband," I say to Torch. We are in the bathtub together. My back to his front. His legs on either side of me. His hands on my stomach.

"I love you, too." He kisses the back of my head. I close my eyes, smiling, the butterflies swarming in my stomach.

"I can't imagine life without you," I confess. I grab his arm and rub my hand up it. Veins protrude his skin. I feel his dick harden at my back.

"You are everything I didn't know I needed."

At his words my heart starts pounding in my chest. I feel as light as a feather. I'm on cloud nine.

"Torch?"

"Yeah?" he answers, and I smile to myself.

"Make love to me."

He stops moving. "Done."

He stands up in the tub, taking me with him, then dries me off quickly before he takes my hand and leads us back to the bedroom. I feel the bed hit the back of my legs and lie down on the bed.

His hands move down my body, letting me see through his touch. He knows exactly what I need. His hands are now at my hips, then down my legs and to my feet. He lifts both of them and spreads my legs.

I feel his breath on my pussy and clench in anticipation.

His tongue swirls around my clit, and I moan loudly. He does it again, slowly.

Torch

I watch as she comes apart on my tongue, her whole body shaking, her toes curled under. And those deep, throaty moans. I pick her up and move her up the center of the bed.

Once I've got her situated, I climb between her legs while she hooks one leg onto my hip. I look down at her face. She can't see me, but I see her. All of her. Her lips, her beautiful eyes, her rounded cheekbones. Her heart, her laugh, that smile she smiles that drives me crazy. She is beautiful, and it's a shame she doesn't know how much so, because my words will never be enough.

When I brace myself at her entrance and push inside, her eyes roll back into her head and her hands lift to my shoulders, her fingers digging in. I move down so I am on my elbows on either side of her face, pressing my lips to hers while moving in and out of her slowly.

I stop and twist my hip before moving back inside again. Her legs tremble, and I reach down holding the one on my hip.

"Are you close, baby?"

"Yes." She grips the sheets by her head. I feel her stiffen, so I reach down and stroke her clit. Her pussy tightens before detonating, spasming around my cock.

I move inside of her swiftly and come right along with her then pull out and move to the side, holding her in my arms. Her head settles on my chest. I tighten my arm around her while her hand runs up and down my side.

"Love you, Torch."

My eyes close at those words. I don't deserve her. "I love you, too, wife." I poke her in the side and she laughs.

"Yeah, you got me knocked up on the first try." She laughs and moves over onto her back.

"That's right," I gloat and move onto my belly, my head on her shoulder. My hand goes to her stomach and I close my eyes, holding my world in my arms.

Kayla

"Kayla!" Jean yells as I walk into the clubhouse. Torch has a meeting or something, so I'm spending the day with the girls.

"Jean." I laugh and hug her back once she wraps her arms around me. "How's the bean growing?" I pat her stomach.

"Morning sickness is killing me." She shutters. I understand all too much. Morning sickness is a bitch.

"Come on, the girls are in here." Jean takes my hand and I follow behind her. I hear voices and laughter. She stops me, and then I feel something tugging on the bottom of my shirt.

"Mia wants you to pick her up," Jean explains.

"Who is Mia?" I ask as I bend down. I touch the little girl's arms and slide my hands down them until I reach her armpits. When I pick her up, she immediately cuddles up close to me. I touch her little face with my hand. She is so sweet.

"Myra and her daughter, Mia, are staying with Ryan for a while. They needed protection," Jean says. I can hear the amusement in her voice.

"Like that's the only reason." I laugh as she leads me over to the table where the rest of the girls are.

"I can take her from you," Myra says. Well, at least I assume it's her.

"No, it's okay." I smile. Mia lays her head on my shoulder, holding her little blanket.

"She is so sweet," I tell Myra as I shift the girl in my arms.

"That little girl isn't shy one bit. She will go to anyone, man or woman. If she wants to be picked up, she will reach for the next person or whoever she wants." I can hear the adoration in her voice.

"You are staying with Ryan, huh?" I ask her with a small smile.

"Yeah, he insisted. He brought Mia into it, so I couldn't help but say yes. I want her safe." I feel a hand run down Mia's head and know it's Myra.

"Mia," Ryan says in his deep, gruff voice. When the little girl in my arms moves and starts to squirm, I let her down onto the ground and hear her running. "I'm going to get her some ice cream. Let you have a break with the girls."

"Bite, bite," Mia says. Her little voice is so cute.

"Yes, baby girl, bite." I hear a sound like someone kissing something, then the girls aww. Ryan must have kissed Mia.

The door shuts. "You are fucked," Jean tells Myra, and I laugh because yeah, she is.

"What do you mean?" she asks hesitantly.

"That man has claimed you as his, though you don't know it yet. He wouldn't be as invested as he is if he didn't want you to be his woman," Jean explains. I nod along with her. These guys are a special breed.

"Ryan is hot, I have to admit; and my poor ovaries explode every time he holds my daughter or does something sweet." You can hear the innocence in her voice.

"Hang on for the ride, girl, because that man will make you the happiest woman imaginable. They may look gruff, but for us, they are softies. They won't ever admit that, though," I pitch in and smile thinking about Torch.

"She's right," Jean agrees.

"Second that," Chrystal says.

"The sex is off the wall, too," Jean says in true Jean fashion. I laugh and the others join.

"Aww, she's blushing," Jean teases. "We all know you've had sex. You have a daughter to prove it."

Myra clears her throat. "Well, I wouldn't call it sex. More like three thrusts and it's over."

I know the sex she is talking about and make a sound of disgust. "At least tell me he made up for it in other ways?"

"No," she says meekly.

Poor girl, but then again, I know all too well. Well, not anymore, but you get my drift.

"Aw, he didn't?" Jean asks her. "Aww, poor you. There is nothing worse than a guy who only cares about himself. Oh, I forgot. I never had anybody before my man. Oops."

I burst out laughing again.

"I think I already love you guys," Myra says through her laughter.

"Back at cha," Jean replies.

"If you ever need a babysitter, I can do it." I'm home all day anyway.

"Thank you! I may take you up on that sometimes. I got a job at a new clinic."

"Welcome, babe."

I hear the door open and then the sound of little feet hitting the floor. "Mommy," Mia says, and then I hear Myra kiss her.

"You're a sticky mess, little girl," Myra says. Mia giggles.

I will be a mom soon.

A mom.

It's hard to believe. When I touch my stomach, a hand covers mine. Torch.

"Husband." I smile.

"Wife." He pulls me up from my seat and into his lap.

"I got a doctor's appointment next week. Gender reveal," I remind him. I go to Chrystal's sister now.

"Okay." He kisses my temple. I kiss his cheek.

"You guys are so cute. My heart can't take it," Jean says, and I smile.

Later that night

"Why is your phone constantly going off?" Torch asks. I sigh and pull a pillow over my face. My mom hasn't stopped calling me all day long every ten minutes. I hear my phone slide against the coffee table.

"Why is your mom calling?" he asks. I shrug. I haven't answered it. My father was going to sell me and my mom was going to help!

The phone starts going off again, and I groan out loud. I hate it; it's torture. I don't want anything to do with her, but then the little girl in me wants her mom.

"Want me to answer it?"

I nod, and a second later he says, "Hello."

Pause.

"She's resting."

It's silent. I sit up and touch Torch's forearm. "Why should I believe you this time?"

Another pause.

"You have put my woman through so much already. She is pregnant and doesn't need the stress."

The pause is longer this time.

"Take a bus, and we will take you to the center. That's it. I'm sorry, but you were going to let her dad sell her. You were basically going to let it fucking happen. My empathy for you isn't great right now. Take a bus to Raleigh, and I will pick you up by myself," he growls into the phone angrily. I hide my face again, hating this.

He hangs up and I sit in silence. "She is going to the center, and that is that. I won't allow her to upset you or put you in jeopardy."

I nod and rest my head against his shoulder. "Let's go to bed." He stands up and takes me with him. We walk hand in hand up the stairs. Once we enter the bedroom, I strip out of my clothes and walk to the dresser to grab my hairbrush.

"Let me." Torch's bare stomach touches my back.

"Okay." I smile and sit down onto the bed. He comes up behind me, his legs on either side of me, and runs the brush through my hair slowly. I close my eyes.

"I can't believe you are brushing my hair."

He stops before continuing. "I want to show you how much I cherish you, baby. Whatever is happening with your mom won't affect you or us. This is a small act to show how much I care about you."

"Torch," I whisper, because this man is so much more than I ever imagined. "You're so sweet," I gush.

"Only to you, babe." He kisses the back of my head before he starts brushing my hair again.

I love this man so much. I have never been treated like this in my life. Torch has made me so happy. I wouldn't change my life one bit, because this life is exactly what I want.

Torch looks gruff on the outside (according to Jean), but he is anything but that with me. I see the other side of him. He is a total caveman but handles me like glass.

fifteen

Kayla

"You are having a boy!" Chrystal's sister says as she runs the wand over my stomach.

"That's right," Torch gloats. I roll my eyes. He bends down and kisses me on the forehead sweetly.

"You have made me the happiest man alive. I love you, sweetheart."

This man...

"I love you, too, Torch," I whisper back to him, kissing him on the cheek.

Tonight is the MC party with the other chapters. We are heading over right after the appointment, because the brothers need to be there before they start arriving. I have my 'Property of Torch' cut on and was warned to not take it off so the men know whom I belonged to.

Torch was right when he predicted I was having a boy. Paisley is still at college, living it up. Not that she told her father that. She is enjoying her freedom after what happened to her at the school and her dad kept a prospect on her until she left.

Human trafficking is a horrible and unbearable thing to think about. It happens to a lot of girls and is one of my worst fears. The gang that kidnapped Sydney consists of traffickers. I don't know all the details, but I know the MC was involved in her rescue.

I can't imagine how terrified she was, though I know she was rescued before anything could happen to her.

"All right, I will see you in a few weeks!" Chrystal's sister says. I wipe my stomach off, sit up, and Torch lifts my shirt over my small baby bump before he helps me down.

"Thank you!" I tell the doctor

"No problem," she replies. Torch and I walk out into the waiting room that is filled with babies crying and women talking amongst themselves. When we step into the room, everyone quiets. We can't look that scary, but my guess, it's the cut.

Torch wraps his arm around my waist. I put my hand on his.

People perceive things wrong. The gruffest-looking men can be the most gentle and loving men. People who are so judgmental can lose out on a lot in this life, but that's on them.

I hear the whoosh of the door opening and feel the outside heat. It's horrible. I swear the plastic of your flip-flops can melt off your feet. Torch holds my hand as he leads me to the truck. Once we are close, I can feel the heat radiating off of it.

The door opens then the truck starts a second later. The air is on full blast. "Let it cool down a bit before you get in, and I will check your sugar."

My sugar is more stable now that Torch is on me about it constantly. Hypoglycemia is horrible, the shakes, lightheadedness, the stomach pain, the nausea. Morning sickness doesn't help either, because it makes my sugar drop even more.

A sharp whine and bark coming from close by make me jump. *Is that a dog?* That better not be a dog out in this heat.

"Torch, please tell me that isn't a dog in a hot car?" I grip his hand harder, and he pulls away.

"Someone left a Yorkie in the car beside ours with the window barely cracked." I can hear the anger in his voice.

What kind of person would do something like this? I have a dog, and he has become my baby. We are going to pick him up so he can come to the clubhouse with me; he is my protection dog after all.

"Get him out, Torch," I urge him and move closer to the sound of the dog. My side hits the window.

Turn around, baby. I do as Torch says and hide my eyes.

I hear glass break and the small taps as the shards hit the ground. The dog is barking louder now as well as panting intensely from the heat. I turn around, and Torch places the small dog in my arms.

It lies down on my arm. Who could do this to an animal? It's pure torture!

"Let me get you guys in the truck." He wraps an arm around my waist and helps me into the truck. The cool air is blasting me in the face. The dog's breathing is getting slower and more even. I think he will be okay.

"HEY! That's my dog!" a man yells. I grip the dog tighter. He's not getting it back.

Torch

"HEY! That's my dog!" a man yells from behind me. I shut the truck door and turn to face him.

"Oh, I was going to come looking for you," I tell him and take a step closer.

"You w-were?" he stutters, his eyes wide when he takes me in. *That's right, fucker, never run up on a man like me.*

"Yeah, you left your dog in your car in this fucking heat without any air."

He shakes his head no, his hands up in defense. "I should beat your ass right now, but I'm not. You will turn around and walk back the way you came, or I will be forced to beat your ass. Your choice." I pop my knuckles and slip on my cut I took off when I broke the window.

He pales and backs away.

"You keep her." He nods and takes off running. I chuckle under my breath. Pussy, but no way was he getting that dog back, because common sense is something he apparently doesn't have.

Taking my phone out, I dial Ryan. "Hey, man, I saved a Yorkie from some jackass. Want it for Mia?"

I know that little girl would love a dog; and this dog would be perfect for her.

"Yeah, bring her to the clubhouse. I'm already here. Where did you get her?" I hear loud laughter in the background.

"Some asshole left her in the hot car."

He laughs. "You broke the window?"

I grin. "Fuck, yeah. I will see you in a bit. Stopping by the house first. Oh, by the way, we're having a boy."

A boy I will pass down the vice presidency to along to, while Kyle will pass down the gavel to his son. Chrystal is pregnant, too, with a little boy. She is a month or two farther along than Kayla.

"Congrats, man," Ryan says. I hang up.

I open the truck door and climb in. The small dog raises its head when I get in. His mouth is still open, panting from the heat he endured in that car. He will be fine, though. If we hadn't shown up when we did, he wouldn't be.

Kayla is fumbling around in her purse until she pulls out a collapsible dog bowl and pours out some water I got from the vending machine inside of the doctor's office. The dog immediately starts lapping it up like it hasn't had water in a while.

"Ryan is going to take the dog for Mia," I tell her as I pull out of the parking lot.

"Okay." She smiles and pets the small dog's head. "Can we stop and get Mika? I want him to be with me tonight."

"Anything for you," I tell her and catch that shy smile.

Kayla

We pull up in front of the clubhouse with two dogs in tow. As soon as we park, my door is popped open.

"Congrats on the little boy, Kayla," Ryan says and takes the small dog from my hands before he helps me down. Mika jumps down beside me and stands right by my leg, pressed up against me.

I feel Torch come up beside me to move my hair so it hangs over one shoulder, showing the back of my cut.

"Ready?" he asks, and I nod. I grip his hand in mine. I will be ready for anything as long as I have him. With him I feel like I can be me without worry. I always feared the unknown, but now life isn't so scary, because he is seeing for me.

I know all the feminists in the world would scream at me, but I can't help the way I feel. I am not weak. Far from it. I just like the comfort he gives me. I can finally be me instead of always being scared, which I am not anymore.

Mika walks so close to me. I don't even need the leash; it's mostly for show. I hear the door creak open and then the cool air hits me in the face.

"How are you, man?" Someone walks up to Torch, and then I hear the back smacks the men give each other when they hug. He let go of my hand and has it placed on the small of my back now.

"Good. This is my wife, Kayla." He rubs my back and then a hand touches mine. I know it's not Torch.

"Wife? Congrats, man. Thought I'd never see that day. She's beautiful." The guy talking to Torch shakes my hand. I smile politely, while Mika moves slightly in front of me.

"This is Lane. He is the president of the neighboring county's MC, the Grim Sinners."

"Nice to meet you, Lane." I smile again and tuck my hair behind my ear.

"She's fucking sweet, too, man? You landed yourself a gold mine." Lane laughs and Torch laughs along with him.

"I know I have." He kisses my temple, and that's when I hear Jean yelling my name from across the room. I wave for her.

"I'm going to go with Jean." I rise up on my toes and kiss him on the cheek. In return, he fists his hand in my hair and attacks my mouth with his. The crowd around us whistles and stomps their feet.

He pulls away and I blush. I feel Jean wrap her hand around my forearm, leading me away from Torch while I am still in a daze from that kiss. Mika is walking beside me, tight to my side.

"Girl, if you weren't pregnant already, you would be now," she cackles, and I laugh along with her. I rub my stomach. My precious baby boy. I won't judge him for his choices in life. I will support him every step of the way. I will take care of him and love him; and he will have the best life anyone can have. Torch will teach him to be a man, while I will teach him to be a gentleman; how he should treat women and especially the woman he is going to marry someday.

I want to give him everything I never had. Stability, love, a family. I never had any of that. I was fed and clothed, but there is so much more to life. I'd wish for rags growing up as long as I had a caring family. I had my grandparents, but they couldn't fill that void of not having loving parents.

My mother is at the center, though I haven't seen her. I don't want to, because she has hurt me too many times. My hopes were crushed over and over. She says she is going to leave him, but she still let him be mean to me, meaning she is just as bad as him. Just because I have a disability doesn't mean I have to be treated as a lesser person.

"I heard you were having a boy!" Jean squeals. I feel her nails dig into my arm as she shakes it in excitement.

"Chrystal is pregnant, too! She is having a boy just like you." She gets excited again.

I roll my eyes and grin at Jean. That girl is to freaking chipper. "Quit hogging Kayla, Jean!" Chrystal yells and I laugh. Jean stops jumping around and leads me over to the girls, who hug me once I reach them.

"I heard you're pregnant, Chrystal! Congrats on the baby boy. I'm glad my son will have kids his age to grow up with." I hug her again.

"Belly bump!" Jean yells and bumps her belly to mine. I burst out laughing. This girl is too much.

A little hand touches my knee. Mia. I smile and bend down. She touches my shoulders, and I lift her and settle her on my hip. Her little hand rests on the nape of my neck.

"Mia, you are so cute!" Jean coos, and I smile. Mia is a sweetheart.

"Hi, Kayla!" Myra says. I feel her arm brush against mine before she gives me a side hug.

"Hey!" I hug her back.

"RyRy!" Mia starts screaming and squirming in my arms. I set her down and hear her take off running. My guess, Ryan has come back from taking care of the small dog.

"Ryan?" I ask.

Myra laughs. "Yeah, her world revolves around him now. *RyRy* this and *RyRy* that."

"How do you feel about that?" I know it must be hard being a single mom when your kid gets attached to someone else. Though Ryan is invested for a reason; he wouldn't be doing what he is for no reason.

"I like him. A lot," she admits and then sighs. "I don't want my daughter to get attached, but it's too late. I've known him for like what, a week? Yet he has managed to wiggle his way in. I want to get to know that man. I can't help but imagine what if we could be something?"

Footsteps approach from behind me. I don't say anything but bite my lip, having a feeling it's Ryan.

"I like you, too, baby, and I'm not going anywhere. Ever," Ryan says behind us. I cheer on the inside.

Myra gasps. I grin.

"You…you…" she says, and then I hear her suck in a sharp breath.

"Yes, baby, I want to see where this goes, but know this: I will always be in Mia's life." She lets out a deep breath. Then I hear the sound of a kiss.

Then I hear Jean awwwwing.

I clasp my hands together, swooning. I am a hopeless romantic.

"Here, baby, go back to Momma," Ryan says. My poor heart can't take it.

"I am going to fall over," Jean breathes out, and I laugh, because it's like she is reading my mind.

After Ryan walks away, I ask Myra, "That answer your question?"

"Yep," she simply says. I grin again.

Torch

"Come on, man, let's go outside," Lane says. I take one last look at Kayla before I follow him outside. Bikers have lined up the lot yard. Prospects are guarding the gate, letting only in bikers who are on the list. They have to show their ID before entering. No fucker is getting inside that's not supposed to be here.

"Give me a quick heads-up with what's happening. I know shit has gone down with you directly." I prop up against the wall of the clubhouse with Lane standing in front of me. Lane is a scary-looking fucker, if I were the type to get scared of men. He has scars up his face from a knife fight.

"We took out the fucking club in this town and now the next town over, YOUR town, is coming at us. Shot at my wife and hired fuckers to try to break through my gate. This can't go unanswered. They are trafficking girls. They were trying to kidnap Kayla, but I stopped them."

Lane cusses. "Fuck, man, this shit was under our noses. I didn't know they trafficked or I would have stopped it a long fucking time ago. This won't continue. I know these other bikers won't let that stand either. You have a good group here."

The MCs that showed up are our closest allies. They can be trusted, which is what we are doing, because Lane is right; they are trafficking women right under our noses. It's time to stop that shit once and for all.

A bike pulls up to the front of the gate, I squint my eyes and see the guy is wearing a blank cut. What the fuck? The prospect starts yelling and has his gun pulled up. The guy is shaking his head no and pulls out a gun right at us.

Before we can duck, he fires off some bullets. Lane falls to the ground and I do the same. Women are screaming inside of the building. Kayla. Men are yelling around us, and then the door bursts open.

I jump up and look at the man who fired the bullets. He is lying on the ground holding his throat. The prospect is lying on the ground holding his knee. There are splinters on the bulletproof glass. The bullets didn't pierce through but bounced off and hit the guy.

I see Kyle run up to me and look at the man and the glass. "Best fucking idea." I nod my head in agreement then turn around and run past them. I need to see Kayla. When I throw open the door, she's sitting on the ground holding Mika.

I can see how scared she is. "Kayla!" I yell, and she immediately sinks with relief. I pick her up off the ground and hold her to me. She clutches the back of my cut.

"I can't stand the thought of losing you, Torch. You are my world," she whispers to me. It strikes me right in the heart. She means everything to me, too.

"I'm okay, baby." I kiss the top of her head and she nods. Mika is pressed up against her legs still.

"I have to go help the guys baby. Stay with the girls. Don't be scared. I will be fine. The danger is gone." I kiss her again and she smiles. Then Jean walks up to her and nods at me.

Jean has been in the MC world longer than Kayla. She will explain to her that our lives haven't been like this for a very long time, and that it will end now. Them attacking our compound just pissed off a lot of people.

"MEETING!" Kyle roars while the other presidents shout for their guys. We all file out of the room; only the prospects hang back.

Everyone enters the meeting room. I sit on Kyle's left side, the sergeant at arms on his right side. The others stand around the room. It's a big room, so we all fit.

"Those fuckers just shot up my place for the last fucking time. They have shot at Torch's woman and then tried to break into their house, where she was alone! They are trafficking women. We ran them out of our town, but the ones that managed to survive are coming back for revenge, because Torch saved Kayla as they attempted to abduct her right out of the mall parking lot.

"The reason I called all of you is because these fuckers are in your town, too. You deal with them how you please, but it's time I take these fuckers out. I will not have my men and their women in danger. Especially not my kid and Chrystal. I will not stand for it."

The men around the room nod.

"It's time for this to end once and for all. Who is with me?"

Everyone around the room stomps their feet and the presidents nod their heads at Kyle. They won't take any chances either. These men's lives are over. They've been playing with fire for too long. It's time to torch them.

"One week from now we meet here and go from town to town ending this. We ride together," Kyle says and everyone nods again.

"This has been happening right under our noses. And now that you mentioned trafficking, my sister's friend went missing a week ago. They can't find her. We have looked, too, and came up with nothing," the Devil's Renegades president, Noah, adds.

Lane steps forward. "We've had a lot of missing women ourselves, not anyone we know personally, but it's still happening in my town."

The Saint's Sinners president steps forward. "Five thirteen-year-old girls have gone missing in a six-month period."

"Fuck!" I yell, because it makes me think of my baby girl, Paisley, when one of those fuckers attempted to get close to her. If Liam hadn't saved her... He is off in the Navy. She is off at college; it's terrifying to think she is off alone like that, but she will be okay. I have to believe that. If I don't, I will go crazy.

"We will meet here in one week."

Everyone nods and we all shake hands. Kyle talks to Lane and Noah, while I walk out to Kayla, who is sitting down with Mika by her side. That dog was the best investment.

One week from now life will forever change for us. We are going on a dangerous mission, but we are doing it for our families, to keep them safe, as well as for the families of the taken women. This gang is taking over these little towns, and it needs to stop.

Kayla

Hearing those gunshots was terrifying. When Torch came back to me after it was over, I felt such relief. I wish those gangs would leave us alone. It all started when they attempted to kidnap me, which feels like it was so long ago.

When all of the men left the room, it got quiet. So I sit down with Mika, who hasn't left my side at all and has been a constant comfort. Jean is rattling off to Myra, who just says nothing but 'yeah'. Chrystal is quiet.

"I think a girls' night is in order. Strip club, hot men, ass in the face." Jean breaks the silence, and everyone laughs. That girl is someone you should bring to a tense situation; she knows how to break the ice.

"Do you want those strippers dead?" Chrystal asks, and I shake my head. I can just imagine Torch blowing his gasket. Maybe that won't be a bad idea. I may be pregnant, but that doesn't mean I can't go along for the ride. Heck, we are all pregnant.

"I don't think Ryan would hurt those guys," Myra says softly, and I bust out laughing. Ryan is the enforcer. He didn't get that position for nothing. From what I have been told, he is hitting 6'5, is muscular, has a beard, and looks scary as hell; but we all know he is just a teddy bear to us.

"Girl, he is the club enforcer. The club is legit, but he helps protect it; he enforces the law," Jean explains to her

Myra is quiet for a second but then says, "He may look tough and mean, but he is far from that to me and my daughter. Judging someone by their appearance, by how scary they look, is shallow. My dad looked scary, and he was the best man I have ever known until he died when I was twenty-one."

She gets it.

"All right, girls' night tomorrow night! I will invite Braelyn and Jessica, too. They work at the center with me."

"Sounds fun."

"I will pick you up, Kayla," Jean says. I thank her.

"Mama," Mia says, and my heart melts. I can't wait to be a mom.

"Yes, baby?"

"Pup pup."

"We will see the dog here in a bit," Myra says. Then all the men file out of the room they were in.

"Come on, baby, we need to check your sugar." Torch grabs my hand and pulls me up from my seat. "Stay,

Mika." My dog stays where he is when we walk away from him. We walk for a minute until I hear a door open.

"This is my room here. We all have rooms in case we need to crash."

I feel a bed at my knees, so I turn around and sit down then reach into my purse, but Torch stops me. He proceeds to clean my forefinger, load up the lancer, and get out the strips. I hear the beeping as he puts it in.

Then I feel the pin pierce my skin with a click. I jump, and Torch mutters, "Sorry." The meter beeps again.

Your blood glucose is seventy-three points per milliliter.

"Let's get my babies fed," Torch says. I hear him ruffling through my purse putting the meter back in.

Seventy isn't really low, but it's not great either. I stand up off the bed and Torch wraps his arm around my waist after he hands me back my purse.

"Dinner should be set out by now. Kyle had the food catered." My stomach growls at the mention of food. Torch touches my stomach, and I bite my lip trying to hide my smile.

We walk back into the main room. It's filled with laughter and loud men. "Sit here, baby. Just sit directly down. I have the chair behind you." I sit down slowly, touching the chair first. Then I reach forward and touch the table, gauging the distance, and scoot forward.

"I will get your food. Be right back." Torch kisses the top of my head and disappears. I feel people staring at me and bite my bottom lip, feeling uneasy. I don't like being waited on, but I can't see what food there is; and it's really hard getting food off a buffet when you can't see what you're doing.

"You're Torch's woman?" a man asks. I've heard his voice before. He is the new prospect who literally just started last week. Torch introduced us a few days ago. He voiced to me at home that he didn't like him much, saying he lacked respect. He's already on his second chance in the week he started.

"Wife," I correct. "But yeah," I say and rub my hands down my legs.

"Well, why the fuck are you sitting there? You should be serving your man, not him serving you. I would have thrown your ass out a long time ago." Then he mutters under his breath, "You must have a golden pussy." But I heard him.

I gasp and my mouth pops open. He just didn't fucking say that.

"The fuck you just say?" Butch yells. Then I hear a sound as if someone is choking.

"Torch! Get your ass over here. This man just insulted your wife, the mother of your child growing in her stomach."

I hear something break and then Torches voice.

"Take him to the other room." His voice is scary. I'm not scared of him, but in that moment goose bumps break out across my skin. The room is deadly silent.

"Wait," I say and turn to the person beside me. "Who are you?"

"Andrew. Lane is my pres," he says, and I nod. "Take me over there, will you?"

I stand up. Andrew grabs my arm and leads me over, telling me what's in front of me. Then I am moved to another set of arms. My husband's. I know, because his hands bring security and safety.

"Am I directly in front of him?" I ask Torch and hear a bit of amusement in his voice when he says, "Yeah, babe."

"How tall is he?"

"Six foot."

"So three inches shorter than you?" I ask again. My head reaches the top of Torch's shoulder.

"Thanks, babe." I reach behind my back and pull out my Taser.

"Apologize and mean it, or I will fry your dick in front of all these guys."

I hear men wince all around me.

"Get 'em girl!" Jean cheers and laughs.

"Woo!" Myra yells. I just smile slightly.

"I'm sorry, ma'am," the prospect says with a tremble in his voice. I roll my eyes when I hear him say ma'am. People snicker around me.

"Thank you!" I say and reach forward, dragging the Taser down his belly until I reach his pants. I light the sucker up and make him scream like a little girl.

"Never insult a woman again, or ill cut it off," I warn him. Torch bursts out laughing, just like the rest of the men.

Nobody insults me like that and gets away with it. I demand respect. Even if I had been with a hundred men, that doesn't give any man the right to belittle me.

"Put him in the next room," Torch says again when I put the Taser back up before he leads me back to my seat. "Sit your ass down," he jokes and smacks me on the butt. I laugh and sit down.

"Jack, I need one!" Jean squeals.

"Sure, baby." He laughs and I smile.

Every girl needs a Taser. You never know when you need to fry a dick or two.

Torch

Everyone has eaten. Kayla is off with the girls and Mike. I slip out of the room with the rest of the guys in our MC. We don't take lightly to our women getting insulted. Especially me.

Kayla made me so fucking proud by standing up for herself and taking no shit. The guy deserved that and more. I may look and sound soft when I'm around Kayla, but when I'm not and you mess with her? You are hurting, fucker.

I open the room and sitting in the middle is Travis, the fucking prospect. I knew from the start he wouldn't last.

"Look, man, I'm sorry. I didn't mean it." The guy is pale and looks visibly shaken. I hear the guys pile in behind me. The door shuts. The room is soundproof.

"Gag him." He starts screaming, but I just ignore him.

Butch puts a pair of underwear in his mouth. Did he pull those off himself or some shit? I look at him questioningly. He shrugs. Crazy fucker.

The guy is thrashing on the ground. Kyle comes up from behind him and stands him up to fasten his hands in the chains above his head.

I move up in front of him and look him directly into his eyes. "You will face the consequences of your actions, and if I hear you insult a woman again, I will end you."

I step back and punch him directly in the face. His head flies back. I throw a right hook and then a left. His eyes roll back in his head. When Ryan hands me a bucket of water, I throw it in his face. He wakes up, and I punch him in the ribs, stomach, and sides. Then once again in the nose, breaking it instantly. He passes out again. I throw more water on him and step back.

The guys will take their turns. They all issue two punches. One for fucking with the club, the other for messing with the club's property.

After we hit him with water again, we let him down. He hits the ground.

Butch and Vin pick the guy up. Travis stands up on wobbly feet. "Walk him out right in front of all the brothers. Techy, take the girls into the kitchen."

Techy nods and walks out of the room. He'll text Kyle when it's okay to go out. The girls know what we are doing, but they don't need to see it.

"Let's go."

I open the door and walk in front of everyone into the main room, where all the other clubs are hanging out. They look at me when I enter and then quiet down when they see Butch and Vin. Lane and Noah give us a chin lift.

Butch and Vin will drop him off a couple of streets away from the hospital. We didn't do any serious damage.

I sit down beside Lane. "Fucker had it coming."

I nod. "Yeah, he did."

He laughs and shakes his head. "Your wife, man."

I grin. "She's great."

He nods. "I need one of those."

"It'll happen when you least expect it," I tell him. Then I see Kayla come back into the room with the girls.

"See you guys in a week!" Kyle shouts into the room. Everyone stands up and files out of the room, knowing they are dismissed. A week from now, we are taking out a lot of bad people who are haunting our town.

I move up beside Kyle. He looks at me. "To protect the club, our family, our code." I shake his hand, and he pulls me into a hug. This is what our club stands for. Family and protection.

sixteen

Kayla

The next night

"Come on, girl, let's go!" Jean says as I get into her car. Torch kisses me on the mouth chastely before he shuts the door. Then I hear the roar of his motorcycle. The only way they would let us go out was if they came with us but kept at a distance so it would still be called a girls' night.

Jean chats along to herself. Because before I can even attempt to answer her, she answers herself. The car stops. I open my car door and Torch pulls up on his motorcycle beside us. He reaches inside of the car, grabbing my hands and steadying me as I get out.

"I will take over now," Jean scolds Torch and he lets me go. I grin. Torch chuckles at Jean. You gotta love that girl.

"Torch is so whipped it's unreal," she jokes. I roll my eyes. "Like your man isn't? We all know he is watching your every move."

"Touché."

I smirk and hear the door open. "There is a step in front of you." I lift my foot and we walk inside. There is loud laughter, loud music. Jean sighs beside me. "No strip clubs for us. The men are with us, and if we even attempt to look at half-naked men, girls' night will end."

I nod, because it's true. Torch would have a fit if a male stripper attempted to get close to me. We can't even go to a baby store without him telling someone to go fuck themselves and to take their eyes off me.

I love it, though. Who doesn't like a protective man?

"All right, bitches. Jean is in the houseeee!" She yells and draws out the 'house.'

"Jean, this is Braelyn. This is Sydney, Emily, and this is Jessica," she says the name Jessica hesitantly.

"Hi, Sydney, how's book been coming along?"

"Kayla?" she gasps. I hear a chair getting pulled out then her arms wrap around me. "I'm so glad you are okay!"

"Sorry for being so MIA. Life got crazy."

"I get that." Sydney releases me, and I hear her sitting back down.

Three girls say 'Hey' politely before another says, "Nice milk racks. I'm glad mine are deflating now that my baby boy is two. My nipples are tired of hurting."

It's completely silent. Until I burst out laughing. I just found my new best friend.

"Thanks! You have a good set, too. My nipples are like razors right now. I about kill Jack if he even attempts to come near them. Those bitches are too dang sensitive."

I reach forward and feel for a seat, then pull it back and feel Torch at my back. I roll my eyes. "Here, baby." He grabs my waist and helps me in the seat.

"That's all you get. Go!" Jean scolds. I hear him retreat.

"Mine is over there somewhere. He says he's going to let me have a girls' night, but we all know we have a better chance of seeing pigs fly," a sweet voice says.

"Tell me about it, Emily. Kane is over there watching me this very second," Sydney says.

"You got to fucking love it, though. These guys are a different breed. They're protective, dedicated, and fuck good," Jessica agrees with them, and I lay my head on the table, laughing so hard tears are rolling down my face. Dang hormones.

"Yeah, they know how to fuck. Most men are a three thruster, and then that's it," Jean says, and I hear her scooting in her seat.

I nod my head in agreement. "I was with one guy before Torch, and it was awful. Very selfish."

"I have only been with Kane." Sydney stops then asks someone, "Wasn't Isaac your first, Emily?"

"Yep."

"How did everyone meet their men?" I ask all of them, because I want to know.

"Kane was in the military with my brother, Ethan. I had a man following me inside a store. I noticed he followed me when I left, so I called Ethan, but before he could get there, the guy attempted to kidnap me. Kane came to my rescue, since he was right across the street when Ethan called him. Since then, we have been together. I was kidnapped by a gang but was rescued shortly after. Kane and his friend along with the MC rescued me." She stops and then says, "Along with Emily. We have four kids. Arabella, who is five, Carter, who is nine, and the twins are three," Sydney tells her story.

I don't say anything, because I already heard this story. Sydney's story wasn't an easy one, but love conquered all.

"I will go next. I got pregnant by a dangerous drug dealer. I left him, because I saw him do something and was afraid. I moved from city to city until I stopped in Raleigh and started working at the center. I was six months pregnant and exhausted. I met Chase when I was eight months pregnant and was insanely attracted to him. Though I knew he liked me. He told me so." She stops, and I hear a glass getting scooted across the table. I shift in my seat.

She continues. "I had Hunter when my ex showed up. Held me at gunpoint. Chase came in and disarmed him. Ethan handcuffed him, and the jackass was taken to jail. Chase moved me out of my apartment without me knowing while I was still in the hospital."

A girl laughs, and Jessica says in mock anger, "Braelyn, that little shit, helped. So Chase and I were together after that. Not sure how or when it happened. It's like we always were. That's about it. If you think I am crazy, Chase is worse."

"Oh man, call him over!" Jean says excitedly.

"Yo, Chase! Bring your bubble butt over here!" Jessica yells at the top of her lungs. I gape at her.

Jean cackles along with Chrystal. "You get used to it," Braelyn pipes in.

A hand touches my back. I am surprised he lasted this long. I guess when Jessica called her man, he thought it gave him free rein to come over. He pulls me out of my seat, so I stand up, and when I feel him sit down, I sit in his lap.

"You called?" a man says, who I am assuming is Chase.

"Yes, Chase, they wanted to meet you."

"Nice to meet you," he says in a sarcastic voice. Oh man, he is a little shit.

"Chase, I am going to hurt you," Jessica says right before I hear a smack.

"Babe, you just smacked my ass. You know what I do when you do that," Chase deadpans.

"You better—" she stops and laughs.

"What happened?" I ask Torch. I feel him shaking with laughter. "He stuck his hand down her shirt."

"Ah!" Chase yells, then all of the girls burst out laughing.

He answers before I can ask. "She grabbed his dick."

I laugh. Then Jessica squeals. "He bit her tit through her shirt that time." I laugh harder and hold my stomach. I can hear men laughing all around us.

"Jessicaaaa!" He gets louder the longer he says her name. "Ouch!" Chase says.

Jessica starts laughing, and I laugh along with everyone. "She gave him a titty twister," Torch says through his laughter.

"It's official. I'm adopting her," Jean says through her hysterics.

"Woman, you've messed up now," Chase says in a dark voice. She quits laughing, then I hear a chair scooting out. Then her laughing again. Then a smack. She gasps. "Put me down! It's girls' night!" she yells.

"Shush, woman." Another smack and then it's quiet. A door slams shut.

"He carried her out of here over his shoulder," Torch explains as I wipe under my eyes. Torch twists my hair and then pulls it so my head is pulled back. I gasp then his mouth covers mine gently. I reach forward and touch his cheek.

"Whoo, baby!" I hear Jean catcall. I pull away, embarrassed. Torch kisses my temple. I close my eyes. I love him so much.

I sit and listen to the women around me laughing, having fun, and join in while Torch keeps holding me. I feel so secure right now. Happy. Imagine if he didn't come into my life. I wouldn't have any of this.

"Good night, Kayla," Jean says when I climb out of the car. Torch holds my hand and leads me up the driveway. I hear Jean leave along with a motorcycle. Jack must be following her home.

Torch unlocks the front door as I hear the buzz of the gate closing behind us. When we walk inside the house, Mika comes up to me, his nose touching my hand. I pet him and he lies down on the ground at my feet. I lean down to pet him.

"Baby, I'm starting the shower!" Torch calls from upstairs.

"All right." I pet Mika for a few more seconds before I stand up. He walks away, his toenails tapping against the hardwood flooring.

I yawn as I walk up the stairs into our bedroom, where I strip out of my clothes and walk into the bathroom. I count my steps to the shower door, open it, and step inside. I touch Torch's back as I walk inside then go to the other side of the shower, to my showerhead.

I go through the motions of washing my hair, washing my body, and shaving before I rinse off.

"Torch, will you get me a towel?" I call when I'm done before I turn off the shower on my side. His is already off.

A warm hand touches my waist, then I am lifted off my feet. I wrap my arm around his neck and am deposited onto the bathroom counter. A towel moves down my body, drying me off.

"Love you."

"Love you, too, baby." He kisses me on the lips and grabs my calves, pulling me closer to the edge of the counter.

His tongue moving through my folds is a complete surprise. My whole body jumps in shock and from the pleasure. "Ah," I hiss. I lean back and place my hands behind me, arching my back.

His tongue strokes my clit in slow strokes until my toes curl. When his teeth nip at the tip, I jolt with the shot of intense pleasure.

"Ohhh." I throw my head back when I feel a finger touching my entrance and tense, waiting, wanting. No, *needing*. I push my hips forward. His finger moves inside while his mouth closes around my clit, sucking it deep into his mouth.

"Oh my! Torch!" I yell. His fingers inside me stroke my walls. He curls his finger, hitting my g-spot, and I shatter into a million pieces. My arms can't hold my weight anymore, but Torch catches me before I fall against the mirror.

He places my hands on his shoulder then both of his hands cup my butt as he lifts me off the counter and carries me out of the bathroom and into our bedroom. I am set gently onto the bed before I hear him walking around the room. Then I feel him behind me, his legs on either side of me.

That's when I feel the hairbrush against the top of my head.

What did I ever do to deserve someone like this?

I can't help it. I burst into tears.

"Baby...What's the matter?" he asks and wraps his arms around me. I put my hands on his forearm.

"I just love you so much and I don't know what I ever did to deserve you. I am so happy it's almost unreal," I admit and sniff.

"I am happy, too, baby, and I love you."

He starts brushing my hair, while I just sit there with tears rolling down my face. I feel such raw love for him that it's almost unreal and so powerful. I love him with every bit of my being.

seventeen

Torch

A week later.

Today is the day when three clubs come together and take care of this gang problem we have. It also means that Kayla and all of the ole ladies are going underground, where they will be safe until this is over.

I packed Kayla a bag in case something happens and we aren't back until the next morning.

We are starting in the next town over, Lane's town, taking out the rest of those guys. Techy found another house they are staying in. We'll split up and take care of both of the houses the gangs are in.

Noah's town is next. There are three places the gangs are stationed at, so we're splitting into threes. Techy tracked the fuckers by their tattoos on their faces and followed the cameras to pinpoint their location.

"Come on, baby," I say to Kayla and help her from Jean's car, who came and picked her up. Kayla knows what is happening today. I wouldn't lie to her. She needs this reassurance, too, because they have come after her more than once.

I lead her inside of the clubhouse and down the stairs, where the girls will be staying. Only the girls and the guys who have ole ladies know the code.

Paisley will be here any minute. She needs to be here, too, until it's over. My phone vibrates in my pocket, so I check it.

I'm outside. xPaisley

I take Kayla inside of the room that is fully stocked. "I will be back. I'm just going out to meet Paisley."

Jean helps Kayla on into the room.

Kayla usually knows where everything is, but the last time she was in there, she didn't have enough time to count her steps and touch her surroundings.

I walk back upstairs then outside and see Paisley is still sitting in her car. Once I come out, she hops out and runs over to me. I wrap her in a tight hug. I missed my baby girl so much.

"I love you, Daddy. I missed you so much!" she mutters against my chest, and I hug her tighter. Paisley wants to be a nurse, and she has to go to college to follow her dream.

"Baby, I love you, too. Just come back home, okay? Who needs to go to college?" I tease her, and she smacks my back.

"Yeah, well, I enjoy the freedom." She lets go of me and winks. I growl at her. She laughs.

"That freedom better be you going shopping alone!" I suggest and knuckle the top of her head.

"Stop, Dad!" she yells and jumps away from me.

"Hi, Paisley."

She looks up at Ryan, smiling. "Hi, Unc." Ryan practically helped me raise her. We lived together for a year or two when we opened the club.

I see Mia walk up behind Ryan. She looks up at him and tugs on the back of his jeans. "Ry," she says. Ryan's eyes light up and he bends down to pick her up.

"Well, well, who is this pretty girl?" Paisley asks and walks up close to them.

"Her name is Mia," Myra says, grinning. She walks up and stands beside Ryan. Ryan kisses the top of Myra's head.

I grin at Ryan. Paisley's mouth drops open.

"Well, Unc, I never thought I'd ever see the day," Paisley teases and then hugs Myra. "Welcome to the family." That's my sweet girl. Myra's face lights up even more.

"Time to go down!" Kyle yells, and all of the women hanging around file down toward the basement. I grab Paisley's bag, while she is walking beside Myra, chatting with her. My baby girl was raised here, surrounded by family. Family doesn't have to be blood; family consists of the people who would take a bullet for you and love you.

Liam became a full-pledged member right before he left for the Navy. He kept a close eye on my girl after she got attacked, and I know he cared for her, but he needed and wanted to make something of himself.

I hate to fucking say it, but I know as soon as he gets back, he is coming for my girl. If someone deserves her, it's him. Not because he is a good guy, but because he will take care of her and protect her above all else.

The three years I knew the kid, I learned he had a fucked-up childhood until he moved in with Braelyn and

Ethan. Ethan pounded some fucking good values into him. Once he has served his country, he will come home to us and be a part of the MC.

I walk inside of the room and set Paisley's bag on the table when Ryan comes in with multiple bags.

"This door will be locked behind me. Chrystal knows the code and knows not to open it unless it's for us. The building will be locked, the gate as well. Prospects will be outside of the building keeping guard. They will not be inside, but at all the entrances," Kyle explains to the girls, and they all nod.

I walk over to Kayla, tilt her head back, and look into her eyes. I wish she could see me. She may not be able to, but her eyes are showing her love. I kiss her softly, a kiss promising I will be back. I then kiss her forehead and pull her into a hug. "I love you, sweetheart. I'll be back in a bit." I hear her sniff and then she nods.

"I love you, too, Torch."

I pull away and it's killing me to see the anguish on her face. I'm glad she can't see mine. I would do anything to protect my family. This is for her, my brothers, and their futures. The future of the MC. These kids are who will be taking over one day; these boys will be the leaders, my kid, Jean's kid, Kyle's son.

I look at Kyle and Ryan. They share the same expression as me.

It's go-time.

We walk out of the room our lives are in. Kyle shuts the door behind us and locks it.

Walking up the stairs and into the kitchen, we lock the door to the basement, then the freezer door.

"Prospects OUT!" Kyle yells, and the prospects scramble out of the building. "Two of you at every entrance and corner. You let someone get inside, your life will be forfeited," Kyle says in a deadly tone.

They all nod.

Lane and Noah are standing by their motorcycles. They nod at us, and we walk over to our bikes and get on.

The police won't do shit to us, even if we are caught, because we have all the chiefs of police in our pockets. Now, they won't ignore it if we do something horrible, but the moral of the story is we are taking out some fuckers that have been terrorizing and hurting people, taking girls.

Kyle pulls up in front of us, Noah and Lane directly beside us. They lift their hands in the air and point forward. Go-time.

Kayla

We hear them leave. I close my eyes and try to not think of the what ifs.

"It won't always be like this; and this is all for you. Those men aren't the normal kind of men, but when they love, they love with all their heart. They will do anything to keep you safe. The Devil's Rejects have messed with too many lives. Kyle told me they have kidnapped thirteen-year-old little girls."

I cringe at the thought of what could be happening to those girls. Their childhood taken away, their innocence stripped.

"I hope they pay," I tell Chrystal. I'm angry. They don't deserve to be on this earth.

"And they will." I can hear the sinister lilt to her tone.

"I want them out of my life. They had my baby at gunpoint and I shot the person who did it. I want her safe, by any means necessary. These men aren't conventional, but they get shit done," Myra pipes in.

I nod my head, agreeing. I was shot at, almost kidnapped.

I sit here and wait.

"This won't be forever, girls. It's just a bump in the road to your forever," Chrystal ends the talk. Then we wait.

Torch

We stop in the next town over. Lane's. He takes the lead and rides slightly in front of the other presidents. This is him showing this is his town.

Once we hit the middle of town, we split in halves. Half of Lane's men, half of the Souls, and half of Noah's. Kyle is with us, and Noah is with Lane.

We thunder down the road.

The house is located on a back road. I pull my gun out of my vest and click the safety off, noticing the others doing the same. We pull to a stop outside. Butch, Techy, and Trey run to the back, so the fuckers have no way to escape. I climb off and walk side by side with Kyle and Ryan, while the guys of the other MCs and the rest of ours are coming up behind us.

We walk up to the front door. Ryan kicks it in and we charge inside. Spotting a member in the corner with a gun, I lift mine and shoot him directly in the forehead.

Ryan is throwing off a succession of shots. When I see a man coming down the stairs, I lift my gun then walk farther into the building and shoot any gang member I see.

They fall around us yet keep coming like fucking rats. Once there is one, there are fifty.

After what seems like an hour, the gunshots fall silent.

My breathing is ragged from the adrenaline. Kyle touches my back. "We need to search this place for any girls."

I walk down the hallway and see a door we haven't checked. Ryan comes up beside me. I try to twist the doorknob, but it's locked, so I take a step back and kick the door in. It's pitch black. I take my phone out of my pocket and use the flashlight to see wooden steps leading down into black nothingness.

"Let's go." Ryan follows down behind me. I reach the bottom of the steps and shine my light against the walls, hoping to see a light switch, then spot one next to the step.

I click on the light.

The sight that assaults me will never leave me.

Ten-, eleven-, twelve-, thirteen-, fourteen-year-old girls along with some older women are in cages on a cement floor, naked, shivering from the cold in the basement.

That could be my little girl right there.

Rage like I have never felt before burns through me.

"Kyle!" I call, making the girls flinch. *Fuck.*

I hear a thunder of footsteps. A few girls start to cry. "We are here to rescue you." I start to walk over slowly to the first cage when I spot the keys on a hook on the wall.

I grab them and walk over to the cage then unlock it while Techy walks up beside me with a blanket. The girls inside step out of the cage and into the opened blanket, her ribs sticking out of her fucking sides, her hair matted to the side of her head. *Fuck.*

Techy covers her up. Her hands twist in the blanket before she bursts into tears. "Can I go home to my daddy now?"

"Yes, baby, who's your daddy?" I ask her soothingly.

"Lane Evans," she says. Everyone in the room stops breathing.

"Is he the president of the Grim Sinners?" I ask her, and she nods, her eyes lighting up.

"My daddy is the president. My mommy said I couldn't see him, because he didn't want me, but if he is like you, I want my daddy. Mommy is mean, too, so I want Daddy. They didn't hurt me like they did the other girls, because they wanted something from him. Mommy gave me to those guys, because they promised her money from what they got from him," she explains, her big doe eyes staring at all of us. Then she picks up a letter from the top of the cage.

Fuck.

She is Lane's fucking kid? I didn't know he had one, and if he knew, he sure as fuck wouldn't have let her go.

"Kyle." I stand up and look at him.

"How old are you, sweetheart?" Kyle asks and bends down to her eye-level.

"Eight."

I close my eyes and grit my teeth.

"What's your mom's name, sweetheart?"

"Marie."

"I'm going to go call your daddy now," Kyle tells her, smiling.

Kyle

How can Lane have a fucking kid? Maybe it was a one-night stand? Holy fuck. No. Lane was in a relationship with this woman for like a month until her true colors came out. He got rid of her once he saw she was stealing from him and used heroin. He walked in on her shooting up.

He walked right out of her life and never looked back.

That was nine years ago. He was just straight out of basic training.

Fuck, man.

I dial Lane. I hate to fucking tell him we found his daughter in the bottom of that basement and was planned to be used for ransom.

"Everything go okay?" Lane asks as soon as he picks up.

"Yeah, man, but I have to tell you something," I say and pace in front of the house.

"What is it, Kyle?" Lane asks in a deadly calm voice.

"There is a little girl down here in the basement who's is eight years old, saying she is your daughter and her mother's name is Marie. They were planning on using her for ransom. Marie handed her over to these fuckers."

"I have a daughter?"

"Yeah, man, I guess so."

"FUCK!" he roars.

"I'm on my way there now. If she is my kid, I will know." He hangs up, and I put my phone in my pocket.

I walk back downstairs and look at all the little girls. Torch has taken his shirt off and gave it to Lane's daughter. Now that I take a good look at her, I realize she looks exactly like Lane. Dark brown hair, with the same cowlick at the top of her head, her green eyes, the cleft chin; she even has the same nose as him. Fuck, she's his kid.

"Jack, load the girls up and take them to where the police are waiting for them."

"Come on, ladies," Jack says to the girls, and they follow behind him.

Torch grabs another blanket off the wall and wraps it around the girl named Tiffany. Her name is Tiffany. She holds it tightly around her. "I'm going to take you upstairs, but you have to close your eyes, okay?" She smiles and says, "Okay."

Because someone is coming to meet you.

Torch

We are all left reeling at the little girl. She looks exactly like Lane now that we know there could be a possibility she's his kid.

Kyle picks her up and covers her head with a blanket so she won't be able to see all the bodies that are littering the floor.

We walk outside, where I sit down on the edge of the porch. Kyle sets Tiffany down, and she walks over to me to sit down beside me. I wrap my arm around her instinctually. She hides her little face in my chest. I tuck the blanket tighter around her.

"You think he will like me?" she whispers. I look down at her. All I can see is her green eyes.

"Yes, baby, I know he will," I reassure her, and that's when we hear a motorcycle and see him flying up the drive.

I step down from the porch and onto the ground. Tiffany is now completely hiding her face.

Lane pulls to a stop and gets off his motorcycle. He looks at all of us and then the little girl. Once he sees her, he doesn't take his eyes off of her.

"Come on, sweetheart." I turn to Tiffany and help her off the porch. She looks up at me and then at Lane, who stops dead in his tracks. He takes a few steps to her before falling down to his knees.

"That's my daughter," I hear him whisper. Then Tiffany drops the blanket and runs over to him but stops when she is in reach.

"Come here, baby." He reaches forward and pulls her into a hug. She wraps her arms around his neck and starts to cry. I look down at the ground, because I couldn't imagine not raising my daughter and missing out on so much of her childhood; and this little girl hasn't had a good one so far.

"Can I live with you now? I don't like Mommy's house," she asks him. I look up at Lane. His face is filled with fury.

"Yes, baby, you won't ever have to see her again," he promises; and he means it.

"Okay," she whispers.

"Can we go home now?" she asks again, and Lane looks at all of us.

"The guys left before you came to go join Noah. He is taking out his town now. We thought it might be a good idea if we stayed behind and helped you."

"Thanks, man. I need to get her some stuff, clothes. Fuck, what do little girls need?"

"Let me call Myra. My woman. She is a doctor. I can get her to pick up some stuff on the way. I will go back and get her," Ryan offers. Lane nods and then picks up his daughter, holding her to him.

"I'm going to take her home now. Meet me there? My VP, Sergeant at arms and enforcer will be around also. We have to take care of the Marie situation," he says, and we all nod.

Marie needs to stay away. She won't be hurt, but she won't be back in that little girl's life.

Ryan climbs on his motorcycle and is off.

"She will be fine. She is underweight and will need a lot of hot, hearty meals, but is otherwise okay physically. She hasn't been fed a proper meal in a long time," Myra explains to Lane. "Eight-years-olds don't need as many things as small children, but we'll need all the necessities. Clothes, shoes, bathing products."

Lane looks lost and almost afraid. "Hey, man, I raised Paisley alone since I was eighteen. I can help you." I pat him on the back. He looks over at Tiffany, who is fast asleep, clutching a blanket.

"Also, I recommend her seeing a therapist. There is an amazing one I know in town. Her name is Braelyn; she works at the center. You can bring her there, and Braelyn would be more than willing to see her," Myra suggests and pushes a strand of hair off her face before looking at Lane. "This little girl is precious. You're a lucky parent"

Lane jolts at those words as it sinks in he is now a dad.

"I am going to wake her and help her get changed. Maybe you want to take her with you to get some things, yes?" Myra says and stands up from the couch. Lane's house is huge, and he owns almost as many businesses as we do, though we have been up and running a year or two longer.

"Thank you, Myra."

"No problem."

She wakes Tiffany, who then follows Myra out of the room.

eighteen

Kayla

One by one the men return home. When Ryan came and picked up Myra, the rest of us stayed inside the safe room. I held a sleeping Mia, who is sitting in my lap with her head on my chest and blanket tucked under her neck.

Five minutes ago, we were let out of the room and into the main room. I am guessing it's all over. I sit here in silence waiting for Torch. For him to hold me and let me know he is okay.

I feel Mia waking up as she starts wiggling in my lap. I shift her and cover her back up. She stops moving, so I know she is going back to sleep.

"I can take her," Ryan whispers into my ear. I jump for a second but then nod. He moves his hands under her little body and lifts her out of my lap.

"Where's Torch?" I ask him and stand up. I twist my hands together in front of me nervously.

"I'm here," Torch says, and I close my eyes. My knees buckle, and then I am in his arms. I lay my forehead against his shoulder and breathe in his scent.

"Is it over?" I ask him.

Torch stops his hand that is moving up and down my back. "Yes, baby, it's all over." I let out a sigh of relief. No more gangs, no more worries.

"Daddy!" Paisley yells. I pull out of his arms and hear him step away from me as Paisley comes running over. "I'm glad you're okay," I hear her say and smile.

"Yes, baby, it's over and done." I hear him kiss her and smile again. Torch loves his daughter. He raised her alone; yes, he had help; but still, he was the one who got up each night changing her diaper, feeding her, loving her. Fixing her hair, dressing her.

It's hard to believe I got so lucky to have someone like that. With the gang gone, there won't be any more worries.

Or so I thought.

Torch

Later that night

Kayla is lying on her back with my head on her chest. I am palming her baby bump. Paisley is asleep in her bedroom. She's staying until she goes back to college in the morning.

"Torch?" Kayla asks, and I lift my head from her chest and look at her.

"Sweetheart?" I push her hair out of her face and she smiles. If she only knew how beautiful her smile is.

"I would like to adopt Paisley."

My eyes widen at her words.

Kayla chews on her bottom lip nervously, and I push myself up so I am sitting on the edge of the bed.

"I know I wasn't around for the most important years, but I want to be her mother. As much as Paisley would let me," she explains. I can't stop the smile that crosses my face. Kayla is everything and so much fucking more I could have ever imagined.

"I would want nothing more, baby, but ask her in the morning?" I suggest and lie down onto the bed. I clap my hands, turning off the lights. "All right," she whispers and snuggles into my chest. I kiss the top of her head and stare up at the dark ceiling.

"Yes!" Paisley cries and walks over to Kayla, hugging her. Kayla wraps her arms around her while Paisley cries into her shoulder.

Fuck, I can't handle all this fucking crying.

Kayla just asked Paisley if she could adopt her. And Paisley said yes. It fucking hurts that my baby girl wanted a mom for so long and never had one. I wanted to give her the world, but I could never give her that.

Paisley felt rejected for a long time, because her mother didn't want anything to do with her. So I was Mom and Dad. I went to all the Mother's Day dinners at school. I talked boys even though it fucking killed me. I played dress up. I've done whatever I could.

She turned out fucking amazing. I duck my head and look at the ground, my throat getting thick at the sounds of my girls crying.

"I love you, Kay," I hear Paisley say and walk out of the room. I can't handle that shit.

"I love you, too, Paisley."

Fuck.

nineteen

Kayla

I am seven months pregnant. I feel like a million years by this point. The heat of the Texas air and me being pregnant do not mix. On top of that, I feel like a whale. I waddle, and it's not attractive. Well, it doesn't feel attractive.

Man, I need some chocolate!

I push off the couch and walk—or waddle—into the kitchen, where I open a drawer beside the fridge and grab a bar of chocolate. I peel back the wrapper and take a bite. I moan and my eyes roll back in my head.

"Baby, you ready for dinner?" Torch calls as the front door slams shut.

"Yeah!" I call back and tuck the bar of chocolate back into the drawer. Save that for later. I am wearing a flowy sundress and sandals. My hair is falling down my back. I walk into the living room, holding my stomach.

"How is my baby this evening?" Torch asks before his lips press against mine. He starts to pull away, but I pull him back to me. I grab him through his jeans while he grabs both of my butt cheeks, squeezing them.

"If you don't fuck me, I will combust right here," I murmur against his lips. He chuckles.

Did I mention that I stay horny? I can't get enough of Torch.

His hands are lifting up my skirt. Is it bad that I am tempted to get down on my hands and knees right now? Foreplay is great, but I need him.

"Baby, just fuck me! I'm already soaked," I beg. He growls possessively then turns me again and grabs my hands to place them on the back of the couch. He holds on to my hips and pulls me back so I am bent over.

Fuck, yeah.

I hear his belt buckle and then feel two fingers enter me. I shudder at the feel and press back against his fingers, moaning when I feel him at my entrance. I push back while he pushes forward at the same time.

"Oh!" I say and hold on for the ride.

Torch gives me what I want and need. He fucks me into oblivion. My body wracks with tremors as I come twice before he finishes. When he pulls out, I take a step back, my legs shaky, and pat his chest. "Thank you." Then I waddle into the bathroom so I can clean up.

I hear him laugh.

Hey, I did mention I was just horny, right?"

Thirty minutes later, we pull up in front of the restaurant, where all of the club members and the ole ladies are eating dinner. Ryan is married to Myra now. Heck, a month after the gang elimination, they got hitched court-house style like Torch and I. Ryan is in the process of adopting Mia, too. Which shouldn't be a problem, because Mia's dad signed over his rights.

Torch shuts the driver's side of the truck and then my door opens. His hands grip my hips, and he lifts me straight out of the truck. Once I am settled on my feet, he wraps his arm around me, tucking me into his side possessively. I can't help but smile at his antics. Even though we are married, he still has to claim me everywhere he goes, one way or another.

I love it.

Torch opens the door to the restaurant. The cold air hits me, and I could sigh with relief. "Yo, Torch!" I hear Techy yell. We walk through the restaurant. I can feel eyes on me; it's nothing unusual.

"Laaaa!" I hear little Mia yell and smile. Her little hands are pulling at my dress. "What about me, Mia?" Torch says, and then I feel her being lifted as she brushes against my hip. Then I hear her giggling.

"Hi, Kayla," Myra greets me and then gives me a side hug. I hug her back before I pull away. Torch still has his hand on my back. I pull my hand behind him and smack him hard on the butt. "Lead the way, babe."

I feel him jump and hear Techy laughing.

"Damn, the farther along she is, the feistier she gets!" Techy says, laughing. I smirk in his direction, laughing with him.

"Come on, Kayla, sit your ass down." Torch chuckles and helps me into my seat.

The waitress comes and gets our drink order. I sit and listen to the talk around me while rubbing my legs together to ease the ache that is already starting to fester again.

Reaching over, I grab Torch's junk through his jeans. I rub slightly and feel him shaking with laughter.

What am I supposed to do? Suffer?

I feel him moving closer to me. "Baby, you need me again?" he whispers into my ear.

"Yesss," I draw out, moaning. He immediately stands up and takes me with him.

"Where are we going?" I ask.

"To the ladies' room," he mutters and I laugh. Hey, you gotta do what you gotta do.

I hear the door open and then close. Then a lock clicks and I am lifted off the ground. My butt hits the top of the counter by the sinks. I feel Torch's hands pushing up my dress before his hands wrap around my panties and I lift my hips so he can slide them down.

My lower body jerks at the touch of his fingers between my folds. I brush his shoulders and feel him lower his body until he is kneeling on the ground. His hands glide up from my calves to my thighs. My body is shaking with pent-up anticipation.

His breath on me, and my legs start shaking. I am burning alive!

When his tongue moves through my lips, my body starts shaking worse. Torch wraps his arms around my waist to hold me up. My legs go on either side of his shoulders then his mouth wraps around my clit and sucks.

"Oh my god!" I cry out at the pleasure. It's almost too much.

Two fingers enter me. He curls them and moves up my walls. I jolt as he touches my g-spot and then suckles harder on my clit. I throw my head back yelling as I come, my body jolting with every pulse and tremor.

As I come down from my high, Torch gets up and presses my head to his chest.

"You almost killed me there." I laugh and pat his butt.

He laughs out loud and kisses the top of my head then steps back and helps me put my panties back on. "I think I'll keep you pregnant all the time if you're going to be like this. A sex fanatic."

I laugh and shrug my shoulders.

He helps me down from the sink. I grab his belt buckle, ready to return the favor. "Baby, when we get home. You're not getting on your knees, and especially not in a public bathroom."

I gape. "But you did?" I question and feel his hand on my cheekbone. I tilt my head to the side, leaning farther into his touch.

"Baby, you're my wife. I gave you what you needed. I will always do that. I don't expect anything in return."

I shake my head with a smile on my face. I love that man.

"Let's get back to dinner." He takes my hand and leads me out of the bathroom. All the talking stops once we step out.

I widen my eyes. *They didn't hear us, did they?*

"The fuck you looking at?" Torch growls. I move a little closer to him.

"Whoa, baby!" I hear Techy yell. *Oh my god, they did.* Ground, swallow me up. But I was desperate.

Torch leads me back to the table, where I sit down. I rub my burning cheeks while I hear someone laughing. Myra. She is sitting beside me. I turn toward her. "Did they hear?"

She laughs louder. "Oh, yeah. They were going to call the police until Ryan scared the waitress to death."

Torch kisses my burning cheek. I smile at him.

Everyone is silent, while I gnaw my bottom lip nervously.

"You're a lucky bastard, Torch," Techy says, and I can't help but smirk at him.

"Don't I know it," my man agrees and kisses my temple. All that sweetness. I can't handle it. I start to tear up. Damn pregnancy hormones.

"Aww, she's leaking, Torch!" Techy pouts, and I laugh wiping my tears.

"It's okay. She does that." Torch says nonchalantly. He didn't just say that. I reach over and grab both of his nipples and twist.

"Ouch!" he says and pulls away. I smile triumphantly and take a drink of my water.

But when I feel Torch moving closer to me, I brace myself. His breath brushes my ear before he starts talking.

"You'll get it later for that," he whispers. I grin.

I sure hope so.

Torch

During the rest of the dinner, Kayla slowly tortures me. She 'accidentally' brushes her hand against my dick again and again.

Once we're done, I stand up and grab her hand. She stands up smiling. That's when I see the fucking waiter who's been eyeing Kayla and the other women all night.

He walks past me, stops in front of Kayla, and presses something into her free hand.

He didn't just fucking do that in front of me. She has her cut on her back, my ring on her finger, and a baby in her stomach.

"Baby, I need to go take care of the check. Ryan and Myra will walk you out, yeah?"

She smiles and nods. I look over at Ryan, who is smirking at me. Hey, a man's gotta do what a man's gotta to do. No guy is going to disrespect me like that.

Myra walks over and takes Kayla's hand. Ryan has Mia asleep on his shoulder with a blanket tucked around her.

Once I see Kayla is outside, I walk to the front and pay for our meals. That's when I see the waiter going into the men's room. I take my receipt and put it back into my pocket then enter the men's room and lock the door behind me.

The waiter turns around and looks at me.

I smile.

He pales and backs up closer to the wall.

"You wanted my woman to call you?" I ask and walk closer to him.

He shakes his head no.

"Then what's this?" I show him the note with his number on it.

"I'm sorry!" he cries out. But he is not. He's trying to save his ass.

"Oh, that makes it better," I say. The guy looks at me, hopeful. "Really?"

I chuckle. "No." Then I bring my fist back and pop him on the mouth. He falls to the ground, holding his mouth. When he brings his hand back, I see a tooth.

"Oh, I'm sorry. My hand slipped. Let me take a look." I tsk at him and pull his hand away from his mouth, take the note, and stuff it in his mouth. Then I force his mouth shut and pat his jaw.

"Now, don't ever poach on another man again. Understand?" I peer into his eyes and he nods.

"Good." I stand up and walk out of the bathroom, the door slamming shut behind me. I walk right out of the restaurant and into the parking lot, where I see Kayla standing by our truck with Ryan and Myra.

"Ready to go home, baby?" I ask once I reach them.

"Yeah, but let's stop and get some tacos for later," she suggests before I help her into the truck. She buckles up and I shut the door. Ryan looks at my hand and laughs. "Man, he was staring at your woman the whole entire evening, too." His eyes widen. "He was?" I nod. "Yeah, but it's over and done now. He won't be eating solid foods for a while." I wink and walk over to the driver's side. Ryan winks back at me and gets into his truck.

"Oh, wait, no tacos. I want some pizza for later!"

I laugh and kiss her. "Whatever you want, baby."

"Well, I want some of your cock later, too." She smirks at me.

I laugh and shake my head. Best thing I ever did was getting her pregnant.

twenty

Kayla

One month later, eight months pregnant.

"The buzzer for the gate keeps going off!" I yell and get off the couch. I click the button, so I can talk to whoever is at the gate. "Who is it?"

"It's me. Your mom."

I let go of the button and back away from it. *Why is she here? What does she want?*

Why does she keep on doing this to me? I want to be in her life, but being in her life causes me more pain than not. I want nothing more than to have my mother around for my delivery, baby shopping, and all that.

I walk back toward the panel on the wall and click the button so I can talk. "What do you want?" I ask her. My body is already jittery with nerves.

"I just wanted to see you. To apologize."

I close my eyes at her words. Then I sigh and bang my head against the wall next to the panel, and I reach up and push the button to unlock the gate.

I have a watch phone now, since I can't seem to keep up with my phone. I click the button to call. "Call Torch," I say into the watch and hear it ringing.

"Hey, baby," Torch answers, and I can't stop my smile.

"My mom is here and I decided to let her in the gate. Will you come home to be with me?" I need him here. I just need him.

"I will be home soon," he says, and I sigh in relief.

"Love you."

"Love you, too, baby," he says, and I smile again. That's when I hear the knocking at the front door.

"She's here."

"Want me to stay on the line?" he asks.

"If you want. But I will put it on mute so you can't be heard, okay? But you can hear me," I explain, to which he mutters, "Okay."

I walk to the front door and open it. "Hi, baby," my mom says once the door is open. I step away from the door and she walks inside. I smell her as she breezes past. Then the scent of smoke hits me.

No.

That's what my dad always smelt like. He isn't here. She may have been around him earlier.

"Mom, do you need something?" I shut the door as I ask her, ignoring the warning signs ringing in my head.

"I just wanted to see you," she says. Then she wraps her arms around me. I leave my arms hanging at my sides. It feels wrong for her to be hugging me. I can't remember the last time she has hugged me like this.

"Okay," I say, confused, and push at her shoulders until she lets me go. My skin is crawling from the feel of her touching me. This woman has done so much or let things happen to me. It's going to take a lot more than a hug or empty words to get me to trust her.

I walk into the living room and click the button to lock the gate.

"Why are you doing that?" she asks, and I hear a tremor in her voice.

"What do you mean?" I ask, confused. "I'm just locking the gate."

What is she planning? I knew she wasn't up to any good.

"Mom, what are you really doing here?" I cross my arms over my chest and put my back to a wall so no one can sneak up to me.

"You sure have a big house. How loaded is your man?" I can sense her walking around the room, hear the things on the counter getting moved around.

I knew there was a reason for her being here, and it sure as heck isn't for me. I rest my head against the wall behind me and close my eyes.

"Just leave, Mom."

"Why would I do that? I am your mother!" she gasps and acts like I just broke her fragile heart. That woman doesn't have a heart.

"Because you aren't getting any money from me."

I hear her stop walking and hold my breath, wondering what's going to happen next.

"That's where you are wrong."

That voice has me ready to hit the ground. It's my father's voice. When did he get here? Panic shoots through me, and I back away from the voice.

"What are you doing here?" I ask, my voice trembling

Breathe, Kayla! Breathe! Torch is on his way here and will be here any minute.

"I sold you, remember? Since you rode off with the fucker, I couldn't find you and had to give the money back!" he grounds out angrily. I tremble harder. My legs are barely able to hold me up.

My dad touches my shoulder right before I feel his breath in my face. It stinks of rotten eggs and God knows what. "Now, I got to fucking do a ransom so I can get some fucking money. It seems to me that your man is rich. Hmm," he draws out, and I touch the wall behind me and pray to God Torch will get here on time.

The panic I am feeling now is something I haven't ever felt before. My father is crazy. I fear for my baby. I fear for my life. I can't even see what's in front of me. I am terrified.

"Now, let's fucking go before that fucking man of yours comes home!" My dad yells into my face. I flinch and close my eyes, breathing in deeply through my nose and out of my mouth. I have never felt as helpless in my life than I do in this moment. I can't run away, because I can't see! I can't fall, because it may hurt my baby.

I grip my stomach with both of my hands, cradling it

A hand twines into my hair and my head is bowed to the side as he pulls it. I stumble after him and then feel my mother at my side. She grabs my hand and leads me to a point. I hear my front door open and then feel the heat of the Texas air.

I hold on to my mother as we descend the stairs, repulsed by the idea of touching her, but I have to. My head is still yanked to the side as he pulls.

"Get your ass in the car!" he yells and lets go of my hair, but not before taking a few strands with it. I cry out, and that's when I remember the gate is locked.

I am pushed into a car onto my back. The heat is stifling in here. I put my hands out in front of me, gauging my surroundings. Two doors open and close. Then the car starts up. What can I do to get free?

I start crying and pray.

Torch

The moment she started crying, my heart turned stone cold. Her dad is beyond dead. He is going to suffer, over and over again. One day for every tear she is shedding. I am still on the phone with her, and the watch she has for a phone has a GPS.

It was torture hearing her scared and her dad speaking to her that way. The worst thing though was hearing him hurt her.

He *hurt* her.

I feel rage like I haven't felt before. Techy is tracking the GPS and is giving me directions through the Bluetooth piece Ryan gave me. They are riding behind me as I race toward my woman.

They just left my property and aren't far.

Kayla

We are driving down the road. I try to control the panic I feel as I hold my stomach and tuck myself into a ball.

Torch will be here for me. I know he will, but I hope he doesn't get hurt in the process.

What kind of parents do what they are doing to me? What they have wanted to do my whole life. My mom pretends to be a good mother, but all she cares about is him.

My father has caused me pain my whole entire life. Belittling me because of my disability, making me feel worthless.

My life was hell until I moved in with my grandparents.

They showed me what kindness was. To them I wasn't worthless. But when they died, I was alone again, which led me to living within myself until Torch. Meeting him was one of the worst and best days of my life.

That was the day he changed my life forever. The day I finally felt, lived, and loved.

He became my rock, my world. He made me see that it was okay to be afraid and that I shouldn't fear, because he would always be there to catch me.

At that thought, I hear the faint sound of motorcycles and let out a sob of relief.

Torch

I hear her sob with relief and know she is close. I look up the road and see a beaten down, old car. *Bingo*. I raise my hand up and point at the car. Butch and Trey shoot ahead of us, so they can get in front of the car, their cuts off, hoods over there face, so her dad won't recognize them.

Ryan and I follow behind at a distance.

We wait until they pull over and then take action.

The wait is agony.

Kayla

I know they are here, following, but my parents don't know that. They are too dumb to figure it out. I sit and wait patiently.

An hour after they kidnapped me, we pull off the road and onto a dirt gravel road. I grab the bottom of my shirt and twist it nervously. I feel light-headed from being so nervous for so long in addition to the fear.

The car comes to a stop then both car doors open and slam shut. I let out a deep breath. I can hear them arguing, but it's not loud enough for me to hear their words. In the car they never said a word. The quiet was unnerving.

My door opens, and I back away from it to the other side of the car. A hand fists my hair and I'm dragged out of the car by it. I grab the hand that's holding my hair to steady myself as I get out of the car to the best of my abilities.

Once I am out, the door shuts. His hand is still in my hair. My heart is pounding out of my chest, while I hold my stomach with my free hand. The other still holds the hand in my hair.

"Just let me go!" I plead, and much to my surprise, he does. He pushes me with the movement and my back hits the car.

That's when I hear a gunshot ring out. I put my hands over my ears and hear my mother screaming, a thump as something hits the ground.

"Brant!" my mom sobs, and I know that one of the guys shot him. I sink down onto the ground in relief.

"I will come with you," I hear my mom whisper and then another gunshot rings out. This time closer in range. My mom just killed herself.

"Kayla!" Torch yells.

I close my eyes at his voice and start crying at the pure relief I feel as I stand up crying. That's when I feel his arms around me. I wrap my arms around his back and grab the back of his cut, clutching it in my hands tightly, not wanting to ever let go.

Torch's body is shaking as much as mine, and I just hold him. He lets go of me with one hand and then I feel his hand on my stomach. Our baby kicks, making me jolt. I sniff and lay my hand on his chest.

"My baby's okay?" Torch asks and I nod.

"I just want to go home," I whisper, and he kisses the top of my head before holding me tighter in his arms.

"She okay, man?" I hear Ryan ask.

"She's fine. Can you call someone to bring a vehicle to pick us up? Along with one of the brothers to bring my bike back?"

"Yeah, man."

"Thanks."

Later than evening

I am sitting on the couch with my eyes closed as Myra examines me. I wasn't hurt and am okay. Just shook up. I was kidnapped, and that fear is something I will never forget. The fear for my unborn child.

"She is fine, Torch. The day is just taking a toll on her," Myra tells Torch when I feel her stand up from the couch.

"Thank you," Torch tells her, then his arms reach under my legs and behind my back. He lifts me off the couch, and I wrap my arms around his neck, my face at the crook of his neck.

I am carried up the stairs and into our bedroom, where he sets me gently onto the bed before I feel him step away from me. "

"Make love to me, Torch. I just need you."

Torch doesn't say anything but strips me out of my clothes before he spreads my legs and moves between them.

His hands run over my stomach. "I have never been so scared in my life," he admits. I close my eyes, holding back tears. "I can't imagine life without you, Kayla." He kisses my stomach. Tears escape and his thumb wipes them away.

His hand drifts down to my leg and lifts it so it's hooked on his hip, while his lips press into mine and I cup his face. When he enters me slowly, I sob against his lips because of the raw pain of thinking I've lost him, the thought of something happening to my baby, and me losing my parents. I miss what they could have been.

"Shhh, baby, don't cry," he whispers against my lips, and I press harder against him, holding his face between my hands. I just need to feel him, all over.

He is now moving, slowly thrusting into me.

"Just feel, baby, feel the love I have for you. Just feel."

I nod and hang on to him.

He makes love to me like it's his last day on earth. Like there is only us in the world.

He is my world.

Torch

Kayla being so upset is killing me. Today was the worst day of my life. Her being scared, me afraid of losing her.

She is lying beneath me right now, giving me all her trust.

Even though I was close behind her, something could have still happened. I have never been that scared in my life. Your world put in danger, the possibility of it being taken away changes a man.

Like the moment when Paisley was attacked at her school.

I hold her face in my hand, and she turns her head to get closer to my touch. Her hands are moving up and down my back.

She looks me directly in the eyes as if she can see me. I get lost in those eyes. Those eyes convey her emotions better than words can.

Today could have been the last time I got to look at them.

So I make love to her.

If you had told me a year ago I would be married today, with a kid growing in my wife's stomach and making love to the woman who is my world, I would have said you were fucking crazy. I may be a gruff and violent man, but that doesn't mean I can't love someone.

Love is a powerful thing. The moment I had my baby girl, she changed my life forever.

Kayla made my world come crashing down around me with just one look.

She gave me everything I never knew I wanted.

twenty-one

Kayla

"They got one of those instant baby bottle formula makers," Torch says, and I hear him lifting the box into the cart.

I am literally about to pop. I am like one day away from being nine months pregnant. I swear if my child doesn't come soon, I am going to die.

We are getting some last-minute shopping in. The baby room is set up, and for the past week I have been memorizing where everything is.

It's going to be a challenge since I can't see, but I got this.

"Here's that thing you wanted that goes around your waist." I hear him throw it in the buggy.

Torch is trying so hard, and it's a good thing he raised Paisley alone, because he knows what to get.

I lean against the buggy, exhausted. I waddle everywhere I go. My feet are killing me. The heat is torturous. My tits hurt, my pussy hurts, and it feels like I need to shit, but I don't have to shit.

"I think that's everything," Torch says and wraps his arm around me.

He pays for everything before we head outside into that heat again. I waddle along with Torch clutching my back and belly. "Torch, I am very tempted to let you carry me."

We stop walking and he puts the things in the truck. I stand there patiently and wipe the sweat off my brow as I lean against the side of the truck.

That's when I feel the pain. "OWWW!" I scream and hold my stomach. I guess that's what you call a contraction. I brace myself against the truck, breathing through the pain.

"Oh shit, Kayla. You okay?" I hear Torch yell and then feel his hand on my stomach, then running up and down my body, checking to see if I'm okay.

"The baby is coming," I tell him once the pain stops and stand back up.

"Oh shit, shit, shit," Torch mutters under his breath. I can't help but laugh.

"Let's get you to the hospital." I hear him walk away from me and start the truck. Then it's driving off.

Oh my god. He just left me sitting here. I burst out laughing. Then I hear the sound of squealing breaks and then him reversing back toward me.

I hear his door open and then him running. "You forget something?" I burst out laughing again and then immediately start wincing as another contraction hits.

He doesn't say anything, but I am picked up. He sets me in the truck and buckles me up, then slams the door and gets in on his side. The truck speeds down the parking lot.

"I can't believe I fucking left you," he says, breaking the silence, and I start laughing again. He joins along. I wipe my tears.

"I am going to tease you about that for years," I admit and laugh again.

"Shit," he says one single word, and I hear honking.

"Did you just run a red light?" I ask and shift in the seat.

"No," he says without emotion, so I know he is lying.

"Liar."

"Fuck, Kayla."

Torch chokes as I grip his balls in my hand. "You are getting clipped. I fucking swear, Torch."

As the pain eases, I let go and turn my head into my pillow. I have been dealing with this pain for hours. I'm exhausted.

When Torch kisses my forehead, I grip the back of his head. "I'm sorry, baby. It's killing me you're hurting."

"I will be okay," I whisper back.

"Hold me," I ask him and scoot over in the bed. He may not be allowed, but who cares. I feel him climb into bed with me and rest my head against his shoulder. He puts his hand on my stomach.

I grit my teeth and grip his shirt between my hands. "Owww," I grind out as the pain intensifies. Then I get the strong need to push.

"Torch, I need to push. Get the nurse." I bite the pillow and scream into it. It hurts so much. It's like my bones are getting broken.

He gets off the bed and I hear him running.

I grab the rails of the bed and squeeze.

The pain lasts for over a minute. But I still have the intense need to push.

"Let's see how dilated you are," a nurse says cheerfully. Torch is back to holding my hand.

"You are completely dilated." She pulls my hospital gown back down. The next few minutes are a flurry of people. The doctor comes in and is now sitting down below between my legs.

"AHHH!" I scream as I have another contraction. Torch presses his forehead against mine, and I grip his shoulder. "I need to push!" I scream. A nurse grabs my left leg and pushes it toward my stomach. Torch does the same with the other.

"Push!" Chrystal's sister says.

I do as the doctor says, screaming as I push. I feel Torch shaking the longer I push.

"I am okay," I reassure him, and he kisses my forehead.

For the next hour, I hear the word 'push' and someone counting over and over again.

Then my baby is here.

When he is set on my chest, I bring my hand down, my fingers grazing his little head, and I burst out crying. I touch my baby boy as he wails at the world.

"Torch," I sob and touch my baby's little hand before he is taken away.

"You did an amazing job, baby." His voice is cracking as he speaks.

"I love you," I grunt through my pain and tears.

"I love you, too, baby." He kisses my lips.

"All right, Momma, let's try breastfeeding." Torch hands me Trent, my baby boy. I rub my nose up his forehead, smelling him, then pull down my top and free my breast. Torch helps me situate Trent until he latches on.

It's an amazing feeling knowing I am providing for my baby.

I hear the chair scooting in as Torch sits down beside me and kiss Trent on the top of his head while I situate the blankets around him better. Hospitals are always so freaking cold.

I already love my baby so much. More than I thought possible. Life couldn't get better than this. My man at my side, me holding my baby, and our daughter on her way here from college.

twenty-two

Kayla

Two days later

It's time for me to leave the hospital. I am beyond ready. We just signed the discharge papers, and I am now feeding Trent, snuggled up in a swaddle blanket, before I have to place him in the car seat.

Torch is in the bathroom showering. He hasn't left my side since we arrived at the hospital. Club members brought us food, and the girls took care of Mika for me. Paisley is already at home waiting for us to get there.

I can't wait to sleep in my own bed.

"Well, look here," a man's voice says.

"Who are you?" I ask and hold Trent tighter against me.

A hand touches my face. I flinch away.

"I used to be your doctor, remember?" he says and then tsks. He touches my face again. I flinch away scooting farther into the bed. I don't hesitate.

"Torch!" I yell right before something hard hits me in the mouth.

"Shut the fuck up! You're going to ruin it." His voice has a slight squeal to it. I can hear the panic. Panic makes people do stupid things.

The man grabs my face in his palm this time and squeezes. I grab at him and scratch hard enough to draw blood.

"You do know Torch is just in the bathroom?" I tell him through the pain his squeezing of my face causes. I tuck my baby tighter to me and away from the doctor.

A door slams against the wall, and the next second he lets go of me and I hear him crashing into something.

"You just signed your death warrant," Torch says. I shiver at the tone of his voice.

Torch

When I heard Kayla yelling my name, I stormed into her room to see that fucking doctor from months ago with his hand over her mouth. I saw red. That man hurt my woman and put my baby in danger. I hear someone walk into the room and see it's Butch. He grins evilly as he takes his knife out of his pocket and motions for the doctor to walk over. In reality he isn't a doctor anymore. We took that away from him; his clinic, everything.

He shakes his head no and moves closer to Kayla. I take a step forward, ready to beat the shit out of the guy.

I glare at him until he finally relents and walks over to Butch. There's a wet stain on the front of his pants. Fuck man, he already pissed himself. Again. Butch brings his knife up to his face and bops it.

"I got your nose!" He starts laughing.

That man is fucking crazy.

I see something sticking out of the fucker's pocket and reach in, grabbing it. I look at the pills. Fucking date rape drugs. He was going to fucking drug Kayla! I will find out what he was planning to do to her.

"Butch, take him away." I take a step closer so I am looking him dead in the eyes. "I will see you later." He shivers and looks like he is about to shit himself. Not a moment later, I smell the strong aroma of shit. He just did indeed shit himself. Again.

"Did he just shit himself?" Kayla asks from the bed. She is silently laughing.

"Yeah," I laugh, and Butch cackles, too.

"Well, make sure you Tase him in the balls for me, all right, Butch?" Kayla asks then kisses our baby boy on the head, cuddling him.

"Sure." Butch smiles menacingly at the man. "Let's get out of here, shall we? You're going to be a good boy and walk out of here like nothing is going to happen. Like you aren't about to get the shit kicked out of you." Butch nods encouragingly as if the man is a child.

"Damn, Butch." Kayla laughs. I laugh along with her. There's only one Butch.

Butch wraps his arm around his shoulders and leads him out of the room. The shit stain on the back of his pants is hard to miss. When Butch looks back and sees it, he pushes him away. "Gross, man."

"Just walk beside me, and if you run, I will cut off your toes." Butch points his knife at him.

"O-O-Okay."

"Good boy." Butch pats him on the head.

I shake my head and walk over to Kayla, who is now breastfeeding Trent. I grab the car seat off the top of the bed and set it on the table before I sit down on the bed beside my wife and kiss the top of her head.

"Why is that doctor showing up after all this time?" she asks, confused.

"Don't know, baby, but don't worry about it. You won't see him again," I assure her. I notice Trent is finished eating, so I lift him from her arms and unwrap him from the blankets.

"Son, this second is the beginning of the rest of your life." I place him on my chest, one hands supporting his bottom, the other gently holding his head.

"He's perfect," Kayla says and runs her fingers down his face. I stand up from the bed and place him in the car seat, buckling him in.

"Ready to go home, sweetheart?" I ask Kayla and she grins, her smile lighting up the room.

"Beyond ready!"

I help her ease off the bed. She grabs the diaper bag and places it on her shoulder, while I grab the car seat and lift it off the ground. Then I wrap my arm around her shoulder, while she wraps hers around my waist.

Kayla

Later that night

We just laid Trenton down, and I am now soaking in the bathtub. Torch is sitting behind me with his legs on either side of my body.

"How's Momma feeling?" He presses a kiss to the base of my neck. I smile.

"I am perfect; only tired. It's been a long day." I yawn and lean back against Torch. He wraps his arms around me and places his hand on my now way smaller stomach.

"Come on, baby, let's get you to bed."

Torch stands up in the tub and then helps me out. He dries me then himself off quickly before I slip on his t-shirt and stumble into the bedroom. I fall down onto the bed still sore and just feeling exhausted all around. Having a baby takes a lot out of you.

I close my eyes and pull the blanket up over my body then feel Torch climb in behind me. His arm bands around my waist. I place mine on top of his and cuddle back into him.

"Good night, Torch," I whisper.

His lips touch the base of my neck. "Good night, sweetheart."

I crack open my tired eyes. Trenton is crying. We should probably bring the basinet in the bedroom with us. I yawn and sit up in bed then feel Torch do the same.

"I will go get him. Want to get the basinet?"

"Sure." I feel him get out of bed and follow after him down to Trent's bedroom, yawning. I walk straight to the basinet he is sleeping in, pick him up, and cuddle him to my chest.

I grab a couple of diapers, wipes, and diaper cream then place it all in a bin. I am sorry, but I don't feel like trekking across the house every time my son cries. I can do it all from bed.

"Here, baby, I got that. Good idea just keeping everything in our room so we won't have to walk across the hall." Torch takes the basket of items away from me while I gently rock Trent from side to side. He is still crying. *Oh, we need a paci!* I grab one off the shelf by the changing table then walk out of the room and into my bedroom. "I set everything on your nightstand." I sit down on the bed and free my breast, grab my boppy pillow, and lay Trent on it, holding him up with my arm.

Trent latches on, while I run my hand down his little back. Torch puts his hand on my back. I raise my head up so he can kiss me softly before I rest my head on his chest.

Once Trent is done eating, I lay him down on the bed to change his diaper, then Torch takes him from me to get him to sleep. "Go on to sleep, baby. I will handle getting him to sleep." I nod and lay back down, my body weeping with joy.

Torch

I lay Trent into his bed and cover his legs then step out of the room. Every moment we've spent with him, I wish she could see. She constantly touches his face trying to visualize his features. For the first time in my life, I prayed to God for a miracle to happen, for Kayla to get her sight, because I know it's killing her not being able to see our son.

Ryan is outside waiting for me. It's time to make the doctor pay for his actions. He got off easy last time, but the moment I found the date rape drugs in his pocket sealed his fate.

I get in the truck then Ryan backs out of the driveway. We ride in silence to the club, which is only a ten-minute drive from our house.

We are let into the gate before it's locked again behind us. I walk inside and into one of the soundproof back rooms that are basically equipped for things like this. Just ask the prospect, Travis.

Pushing the door open, I see the doctor standing up with his arms in the air. Butch has the guy shirtless, raking his knife across his belly. He's not cutting him, just torturing the man with the unknown. It stinks in here. Apparently, the man has no control of his bowels.

Kyle steps into the room behind me, followed by the rest of the club. The guy had a chance, but he threw it all away, and now he must be dealt with.

It's also about my revenge. The guy fucking tapped Kayla on the mouth with his phone.

"We gave you a chance," Kyle starts and the doctor starts yelling. I walk over and punch him on the mouth. "How does it feel getting hit in the mouth? Isn't that what you did to Kayla? *My* woman?"

"My ha-ha-hands slipped," he stutters as he tries to move away from me, even though his feet are barely touching the ground.

"You are going to die," Kyle says and the guy starts screaming.

"Be a fucking man and man up. You had a chance and threw it away. You should have died before because you touched a woman of the club. But she begged us to spare your life. Bell," I mention her name and watch as his eyes widen.

"She thought nobody deserved to die at her hands. Her man didn't want to honor her wishes, but she never asks for nothing. But not anymore. He gets his revenge along with me." I look him straight in the eye. "Why did you bring the date rape drug?"

His eyes widen and he starts shaking his head no. "Answer." I grip his jaw between my fingers, squeezing with all my might like he did Kayla.

"I just wanted to have some fun. What's wrong with that?" he says through his screams of pain.

"You were planning on raping her?" I ask in a deadly, calm voice before I let the rage take over.

The doctor nods. "Just wanted what was taken from me."

I clench my fists and take a step back, seething.

Ryan steps forward in my place "You molested an ole lady of the club, then you attempted to molest another and rape her. Your sentence is death."

"Please!" the doctor screams. I stick a rag in his mouth before I flip him around and tear open his shirt then step toward the bare wall and click the hidden button. The wall flips over, giving us our toys. I grab my blowtorch. "Butch, cut off his pants and underwear."

Butch does as he is told.

I fire up the blowtorch with one place in mind: his dick. He was going to rape my wife. His screams fill the room for a long time before Allen finishes the job by cutting off his balls and shoving them down his throat.

It's our job to protect and serve justice. That man deserved it.

twenty-three

Kayla

Three months later.

"How's the new momma?" Techy smooches me on the cheek. It's baby city now at the club. Chrystal had her son a couple of months before I had Trent. Jean had her baby boy as well. And Bell had her baby. Myra is pregnant now with twins. Bless her heart.

Trent is squirming in my arms. I know he is hungry, so I grab the baby blanket and place it over my shoulder and down to cover Trenton before I free my breast and he latches on. Trenton stays hungry no matter what. My tits are taking the beating. My nipples are so sore!

"I am wincing over here, girl!" Jean says.

"Your nipples hurt, too?" I ask her and shift Trenton in my arms.

"Yeah, man, whenever Jack attempts to get close to them, I feel like chopping his dick off! My kid has one itty bitty tooth, but let me tell you, he chomps down."

I laugh at her and nod my head in agreement, because Trenton's gums hurt. "Yeah, man, I feel like cutting these suckers off once he's done breastfeeding." Chrystal winces as well, so I know she is feeding her son, too.

"But isn't it the best feeling in the world? Knowing you are caring for you baby? Providing for it? Its most basic need?"

"I never thought I could love something so much. My baby is my world," Jean voices. There isn't a purer love than the love you have for your child.

"The day Mia was born was the best day of my life. I did everything completely alone; until Ryan. Ryan, god, that man." She stops. "He became everything to me, showed me what true love is and what family means. I have a family in you guys."

"Aww, Myra." I sniff and wave her over. A second later she is hugging me. "You are my family, never doubt that." I squeeze her tighter before letting go.

"Come on in, Alisha!" Jean yells and I smile. Alisha is Techy's woman. Well, he met her online and then in person right after I met Torch. He didn't bring her around for a couple of months; she had things to work through.

Her home life was fucked up. She was a skittish mess for a long time. But not with Techy. She is twenty years old; Techy is twenty-four. He is beyond obsessed with that girl, beyond protective like Torch, but it's worse. According to Jean, he won't let her out of his sight

I guess that's because of her anxiety and panic attacks. That girl was trapped in her fucking house from the age of fourteen up until she was twenty years old. Her parents never allowed her out, and she had no way to get a job, because she lived an hour outside of anywhere. But they had Wi-Fi, and she took advantage of that. But being trapped in that house, locked in her room, the fighting, the abuse; it has messed with her nerves really bad.

But not anymore. She is a lot better now, is almost a different person, to be honest. But Techy is still very protective. I was talking to her the other day when I heard a body hit the floor. Alisha asked Techy why he did that for. He answered, and I quote, "He was looking at your ass."

We as women all secretly love that our men are like this. It's their way of marking their territory and it's fucking hot. I know I want to bang the shit out of Torch when he goes all caveman.

"You know I love you, right?" I say to Torch as I lay on his chest after a bout of hot sex.

"Yes, my love, I do." He kisses me on the lips. I sigh then sit up on the bed. I need to tell him something and am not sure how he is going to take it.

"I need to tell you something." I sit with my legs crossed Indian style. I feel him move around on the bed and know he is sitting up, too.

"I got a call from my new optometrist."

I bite my bottom lip nervously because this can either go well or horribly bad.

"What did he say?" he asks cautiously.

"He said surgery might reverse the damage that was done to my eyes."

He sits in silence before he touches my face, tilting it. "What do you want to do?"

"I want to be able to see, and I think it's worth a chance. But I am scared of something going wrong," I admit and bring my legs up against my front to wrap my arms around them and rest my head at the top of my knees.

"Baby, I will support you no matter what you want to do." I feel Torch move closer to me, his arms wrapping around me legs.

I want to see more than anything. To see my husband, to see my baby, to see my Paisley. To see my girls and the guys. I want to watch my baby grow up, grow into a man. I want to see Torch as he makes love to me and look deep into his eyes.

"I am going to do it," I tell him and sigh. I am scared, but my desire to see is overpowering my fear. Though I can't imagine something happening to me and Torch having to raise our son alone. I know he would have help, but I want my baby boy. My heart is breaking at the thought.

"Stop thinking so hard," Torch says, and I feel him rising up to look at me.

"I can't help it." I let out a deep breath and rub my face.

"Do something for you for the first time in your life. I will be there every step of the way." He kisses my forehead, lingering there for a few moments.

A month later

I am lying in a hospital bed waiting to be taken down for surgery, shaking so badly from nerves. Torch is sitting beside me holding my hand. I am so fucking scared.

Myra just left with my baby boy after I kissed him goodbye. That was the hardest thing I have ever done, the thought of being away from him for a couple days.

Then the long process of letting my eyes heal and then the reveal if the surgery worked.

I bite my lip to stop the tears and turn my head away from Torch so he won't see them. I can't stand the thought of him being upset by my tears.

"We are ready to take her down," a nurse says. I let out a sob, unable to hold it in any longer. I feel Torch kissing my forehead and then my lips. He doesn't move for several seconds.

"I will be waiting for you, Kay." He kisses me one last time. I nod. "I love you."

He brushes my hair away from my face. "I love you, too, baby."

I feel the bed moving as the nurses unlock it so they can roll me down the hall. I squeeze Torch's hand before I let go. It feels so wrong to do that.

As they roll me down the hallway, I can hear doors opening and shutting. Then I am brought into the world's coldest room.

Something is placed over my mouth.

"Count to ten," a nurse says, and I open mouth counting to ten. "1,2,3,4,5,6…"

"Kayla." I hear someone saying my name and turn my face in the direction of the voice. "Hmm," I mumble.

"Sleep, baby." I recognize that voice now and reach out my hand. His hand entwines with mine and I smile sleepily. That hand means home.

"Wuv you," I mumble then snuggle back into the pillow.

Torch

I watch as Kayla falls back asleep. I just needed to know she is okay. Now that I do, it feels like the weight of world has been lifted off of my shoulders. I leave her side and walk out into the hallway where the doctor is.

"How likely is it, Doctor?" I cross my arms and brace myself for the news.

"Very likely, actually. The reason she was blind in the first place was from a head trauma she suffered as a baby, which more than likely was from being dropped. She could have been able to see years ago." His face softens when he says the part of her being dropped.

Fuck.

The thought of my woman as a baby, unable to defend herself, being hurt like that, someone so fucking innocent, makes me think of Trenton and Paisley.

"Thank you, Doctor." He nods and I walk back into the room to stay with Kay. I said I wouldn't leave her, and I don't plan on doing that any time soon. I put down the bar on the bed then go to the other side of the room, grabbing the spare bed. I push it beside hers. I want my woman in my arms.

twenty-four

Kayla

Today is the day I can take off the wrap on my eyes. The doctor gave me permission to do it at home. Well, he didn't advise it, but I am doing it anyway.

I am in the living room with Torch sitting beside me holding Trenton. I let out a shaky breath and raise my hand toward my eyes. Then I start to peel off one bandage and then the other. My eyes are still closed.

"Let me see your eyes, baby. I miss them," Torch says and I smile.

I let out a deep breath as a way to brace myself before I slowly start to open my eyes. I can see. It's still blurry, but I can make out shapes and colors. Putting my hand over my face, I start to cry. I can see. I can see! "Baby, what's wrong?" Torch pulls me into him and I sob against his chest.

"I can see." I cry harder and clutch his shirt into my fist. His body stiffens. "You can see?"

I nod and pull back to look at him. My mouth hits the ground as my vision adjusts and clears more and more. Oh my god. He's so hot! He has tattoos running down his arms, dark eyelashes so dark it looks like he is wearing mascara. Ice-blue eyes and a nose that's straight with a slight bump in the middle. Stubble covering his jaw. I look down at his hands and put ours side by side.

My husband.

The man who made me feel.

The man who showed me what love is.

The man who gave me everything I never knew I wanted and needed.

The man who I never saw but loved with everything in me.

This man who is my everything, my heart, and the other part of my soul.

Trenton lets out a sharp cry and I look down at him then start to cry more happy tears. I take my baby from my husband's arms and kiss his chubby cheeks before I lay him in my lap and look down at his face. He looks like his daddy. I look up at Torch then down again at Trenton.

"He looks like you." I grin. He smiles back at me, flashing perfectly straight teeth.

"He does, but he has your eyes."

"I don't know what I look like."

"Let's fix that." He takes my hand and helps me off the couch then takes Trenton upstairs into his bed and is back down soon after. I hear toe nails hitting the hardwood flooring. *Mika!* I look in the direction of the kitchen and see Mika turning the corner. I stare at my dog in awe and then back toward Torch.

While he leads me up to our bedroom, I look at our house. It's way bigger than I thought. We reach our bedroom, where Torch stops me right at the door. Our eyes connect, his face softening as he looks at me. My heart is pounding out of my chest when he brings his hand up to my face.

His free hand goes to my shirt, and I raise my arms above my head. He pulls the shirt over my head. I look at him, wanting to see and memorize everything. Then I bring my hand behind my back and let my bra hit the floor.

His eyes darken as he takes me in. He brings his hand down from my face, sliding it down my neck and to my breast. He looks at me with a dark expression of lust, but softens again with what I now know is affection.

He pinches my nipple and I jolt. His eyes close slightly as he moves closer to me and picks me up off the ground, and I put my arms on his shoulders. I can't take my eyes away from his face.

The bed touches my back. He sits up and pulls my pants down my legs along with my underwear. I move up the bed until my head touches the pillows at the top, watching while Torch strips out of his clothes.

I watch hungrily. His arms flex with his every movement, and his abs ripple down his body. He's got strong, muscular legs. He pulls off his boxers and I stare at his dick. Holy shit, it's bigger than I imagined.

Torch climbs onto the bed and in between my legs. He leans down onto his elbows on either side of my head. I raise my hands and touch his face, unable look away from his eyes. They're telling me so much more than his words.

I raise my face so I can kiss him and close my eyes as I sink into the kiss. I feel his dick at my entrance and lift my leg up on top of his hip. When he sinks inside slowly, I feel him graze my sweet spot and break my mouth from his, moaning, throwing my head back once his lips go to the hollow of my throat.

I bring my head back down and stare back at him. His face is raw with emotion.

I know me being able to see is affecting him, too.

"Let me see all of you, Torch. Let it go," I tell him and kiss his cheek. Torch enters me again slowly over and over. We never break eye contact.

We come together locked onto each other's eyes.

"I love you, Torch." My eyes fill with tears and his face softens. "I love you, too, Kay."

"You didn't tell them I can see, right?" I ask Torch as we pull up in front of the restaurant.

"Nope," he says, grinning, and I smile back at him. I can't wait to surprise them. He gets out of the truck and walks over to my side then pops open my door, lifting me out. Then he opens the back door and lifts Trenton out, carrier and all.

I grab the diaper bag and put it on my shoulder. Torch grabs my hand and we walk hand in hand into the restaurant. Everyone is already sitting down, so they don't see us. "Jack, I swear if you don't quit touching me, I am going to hurt you!" Jean yells. I take in her appearance. She has fiery red hair. Jack beside her is muscular, with one full sleeve of tattoos.

I study the rest of the group, taking in the girls one by one. I see a woman who is around 5'0 holding a little girl. Myra and Mia. I smile at Myra and her eyes widen. I nod

my head, grinning from ear-to-ear. She puts her hand over her mouth while her eyes fill with tears.
"Why are you crying?" Jean asks.
"Hi, Jean."
She turns around so fast I'm surprised she doesn't get whiplash.
"Ha! Your tits are bigger than mine! You lied," I tease and wink at her.
Her mouth pops open then closes a couple times before she starts screaming and crying at the same time. "Oh my god! She can see!"
I nod my head and run over to her, wrapping her in a hug and squeezing. She cries against my shoulder. I blink my eyes trying to stop my own tears. Another set of arms wrap around me, and I see it's Myra. One by one all of the women pile into one large hug. Chrystal, Bell, and Alisha.
"I love you girls."
"We love you, too!" Jean scream-cries.
When we all let go of each other, I wipe under my eyes. Then I turn and look at Torch, who is smiling at me. My life couldn't get any better. I walk over to my husband, stand up on my tip-toes, and kiss him. He entwines his hand in my hair and kisses the shit out of me in response.

"Look at yourself."
Torch has me standing in front of a mirror, naked.
"Look at how beautiful you are."

He is behind me and is looking over my shoulder.

"Your eyes."

His hands drift down to my belly that is covered in stretch marks. "These marks are the most beautiful thing. They're testimony you've been carrying our son for nine months."

His hands move up to my breasts then cup them. "These feed our baby."

His hands cover my heart. "The most beautiful thing about you is your heart. The light that comes off of you makes my cold heart not so cold. You are the kindest person I have ever met and the most loving."

I look up at the ceiling, willing the tears away.

"Torch," I whisper feeling overwhelmed.

"Most of all, I just love you."

I turn around at that and look at him.

Then I grab his face between my hands and kiss him.

My life changed from nothing to everything.

I have a family. A real family. Now I get to spend the rest of my life with them. Raising my son and watching him grow up. Watching Paisley become a nurse and getting married one day. And I also get to spend the rest of my life with my husband.

epilogue

Kayla

One year later

Trenton is crawling along the floor while I am sitting on the couch with Torch. We watch as our son grabs the corners of the coffee table, lifting himself up to his feet. He turns and looks at us. Gives us that slobbery grin.

He lets go, and I watch in shock as he walks over to us, wobbling from side to side, but managing to make it over.

I look at Torch in shock and he does the same.

We both just witnessed his first steps.

I pick Trenton up and kiss him on the cheek. My sweet baby boy.

"Oh, and by the way, Torch, I'm pregnant." I hide my face and grin.

"Kayla! Are you serious?" Torch asks, shocked. I look over at him, nodding.

Eight months later

Torch is holding Rose against his bare chest with one hand under her bottom, the other on her little back. We kept the gender of this one a surprise. When the doctor announced we had a girl, I thought Torch was going to pass out.

If I hadn't been in horrible pain, I would have laughed. I didn't get an epidural to ease the pain, just like I didn't with Trenton. I'm afraid of needles. The thought of getting a shot in my spine and possibly being paralyzed was too terrifying.

"Love you, Torch."

He opens his eyes and smiles at me. "I love you, too, baby."

One year later.

"Happy birthday to you! Happy birthday, dear Rose. Happy birthday to you." Everyone sings 'Happy Birthday' to my baby girl, who is one year old today. Rose smiles and then grabs a handful of cake and stuffs it into her mouth. I laugh at her and then look around the room for Trenton.

Out of the corner of my eye I catch him running away. He's holding a tray of cupcakes as he climbs up into his tree house, where I see all of his friends in there with him. I pat Torch on the shoulder and point. He laughs and wraps his arm around me, kissing the top of my head.

Even after three years, I grow to love this man more every single day.

Trenton starting Kindergarten

My little man is ready for school. He dressed himself, so it's him in a miniature cut and wearing biker boots. If there was ever a child who is just like his father, it's Trenton. He is his father's son.

Torch walks into the kitchen carrying a sleepy Rose. She looks up at me and grins before plopping back down onto her daddy's shoulder. Torch walks over to me and kisses me on the lips before smacking me hard on the butt. I grunt and whip the dishtowel at him.

"Help me, Trenton."

Trenton grins and has a determined look on his face. He runs over and wraps his arms and legs around Torch's leg, hanging on like a monkey. Rose joins in and starts tickling him on the neck.

He fakes being hurt. I laugh at his antics.

When we walk our son into school, I see Jean standing there, crying. Her son is starting school, too, and she is taking it hard.

"You sure you don't want mommy to homeschool you?" she asks him with big, hopeful eyes. I can't help but laugh.

"Yes, Mom," her son, Matthew, says rolling his eyes. He looks around the room and throws me a smirk when he sees me.

That kid is going to be a heartbreaker.

All of the MC kids are way beyond good-looking. I may be biased, but who cares? It was a team effort to raise these kids, because only we would raise hellions.

A little girl walks over with the biggest brown eyes I have ever seen. She lifts her hand out for Trenton. "My name is Morgan. What's yours?"

"Trenton," he says and shakes her hand. He puffs out his little chest. I bury my face in Torch's chest trying to stop my laughter. That's Torch's son.

"Well, my name is Matthew." Jean's son walks up to her and shakes her hand. She smiles at both of them.

"She is too friendly!" I hear a man say and look over. It's Isaac and Emily. I haven't seen them in years!

I walk over. "Hi, Emily. How are you?"

"Kayla! Is your son here?" She smiles at me before hugging me.

"Yeah, he's over there." I point to where he's sitting beside their daughter; on the other side of her is Matthew.

"Torch."

I look at Torch, who is standing in front of Isaac. Torch lifts his hand for him to shake. "Isaac."

I look at Emily, and we both roll our eyes at the same time. Men.

"Trenton, come give me a hug good-bye," I call for my son. He turns around and runs over to me then wraps his arms around my stomach. "I love you, Trenton. Have a good day."

"Thanks, Mommy."

Oh, I feel the tears coming.

He lets go of me and moves to Torch, who picks him off the ground. Trenton wraps his arms around his neck. "Love you, Daddy."

Torch closes his eyes. I know he is affected, too.

"Jack, let me go!" Jean yells in the hallway.

"Bye, son." Torch kisses him on the head before he sets him back down on the ground. Then he grabs my hand as we watch our son walk back over to Matthew. They both sit down with Morgan between them. Trenton grabs her pencil and starts writing on her paper. Morgan takes the pencil from him and smacks his wrist. Trenton sits back up and crosses his arms, pouting. Matthew is smiling at him.

Trouble, all of them trouble.

"Come on, baby, they'll be fine." Torch tugs on my hand and we walk out of the room. I look back one last time at my baby boy, who is now busy playing. Isaac and Emily follow out behind us.

Jean is lying half on the floor, crying. "Jean, I swear if you don't get your ass up, I am going to spank you!" Jack growls, but I can see he is trying not to laugh.

"Promise?" She stops crying and looks up at him, hopeful.

"Yes." He laughs and picks her up.

"Can we have more babies?" she asks.

"No more." He shakes his head no. She pouts.

I turn around and look at Emily, who smiles at me. "It was nice seeing you, Emily!"

"Nice seeing you, too!" She flips her hair over her shoulder, and I see the scars on the tops of her shoulders. Isaac looks at me as I look at her scars, glaring at me, daring me to say anything.

"Bye, Jean!" Torch takes Rose's hand and we walk out of the school.

I tear up, because my baby boy is growing up too fast.

"Mommy, I'm hungry," Rose says sweetly and I look down at her. She is grinning at me with that blinding smile. She is my mini-me. She looks exactly like her momma.

"Sure, baby, let's go."

Torch buckles her in and then opens my door and kisses me softly. "Love you, sweetheart."

"Love you, babe."

I smack him on the ass and he jumps and glares at me, silently saying I am going to get it later.

I can't wait.

Torch

"No!" I yell at Liam. He just asked for Paisley's hand in marriage. My baby girl isn't getting married ever.

Liam smirks at me. I glare.

"No," I say again, glaring.

"Torch, you know I love that woman. I have since I was sixteen years old," he argues.

I huff and glare at him again. This is the hardest moment of my life.

"I will protect her with my life."

I look at the ceiling. Liam saved my daughter's life and kept her safe when…I don't want to think about it.

"I know that, Liam, but that's my baby girl." I look at him. Fully look at him. Liam became a huge part of Paisley's life when she was sixteen years old. He left to become a SEAL and is now the sergeant at arms of the club.

"If you hurt her…" I trail off and take my gun out of my gun belt. I cock it and point it directly at his face.

"You know that's not possible, man." Liam's voice softens. I know that look. I have the same look on my face when I am with Kayla.

"Just love her, man. My baby girl deserves the world."

"Done." He raises his hand, and I put my gun up before I place my hand in his. Giving away my baby girl.

Trenton is nineteen years old

I cling to my baby boy. He and Matthew are leaving to become SEALs. Morgan beside me is crying.

For years it's been Matthew, Trenton, and Morgan. They're best friends.

"I love my son." I tell him as tears run down my face. I pull back to look at him and put both of my hands on his cheeks.

"Kick ass. I am so proud of you, Trenton." I kiss him on the cheek and he smiles at me.

"I love you, Mom." He lets go of me and I curl into Torch's arms, barely able to hold back my tears.

Trenton turns to Morgan. She rushes into his arms and sobs against his chest. "I will be home before you know it." He kisses her forehead then lets go of her.

Matthew steps into her view, and she cries harder. "Don't cry for me, darling." She rushes into his arms and clings to him.

"Come back to me, Matthew. I need you and Trenton."

I turn my head at the sight of them all. Trenton is at her back.

"Bye, Trenton." Rose walks over and hugs her brother. "Bye, sis, don't get into any trouble; and you need to leave that boyfriend of yours." He glares over her shoulder at her boyfriend. I laugh when I see Torch doing the same thing along with Cash, Ryan's son, who is crazy over my daughter, but she doesn't know it.

"I miss Trenton already," I confess to Torch.

"Me, too, baby, but he wants to do this. He has Matthew." He drags his hand down my back.

"Rose will be leaving soon, too." I can't bear the thought.

"Don't say a word," he grounds out.

"Don't forget our grandbabies." I tease and he huffs.

"I'm too young to be a grandpa."

I laugh. Torch didn't like the thought of Paisley becoming a mom, 'cause that meant she's having sex. In Torch's mind that doesn't happen. At all.

"Thank you."

He looks at me, confused. "What for?"

"For giving me this amazing life."

His face softens and he cups my cheeks between his hands. "No, thank you. This life wouldn't be this life without you in it."

"I love you, Torch." I put my hand on top of his.

"And I love you, sweetheart." He kisses me on the forehead. I close my eyes and soak in all that is Torch.

My husband.

My Forever.

The End

Coming Soon
Techy
Ryan
Butch
Trey
Vin
Liam
The kids will have books after this series ends.
Morgan (Book One of the next generation) (She is with Trenton and Matthew)

Sneak Peek of Techy!

Techy

Prologue

Techy

I am searching a dating site for the men who are part of that trafficking ring. I have traced some of the gang members to this site and noticed some of the girls on here have gone missing.

I'm searching a member out, going to his box of messages when she catches my eye.

I click on her profile.

She's fucking beautiful. Green eyes, freckles dotting her small nose, large full lips, high cheekbones, and long, dark brown hair that reaches her butt, the ends curled in a bit.

Why is she on here? She looks around twenty or twenty-one and ripe for the taking by the gang. She would be sold to be a wife in a foreign country or pimped out.

Grabbing my other laptop, I boot it up and log into my account. I message her to make sure she is still fucking alive or hasn't been taken yet. I can see she never messaged the guy back.

I am Techy. I can hack anything. I am one of the original members of the Devil's Souls MC. We are planning to eradicate the gang members that attempted to kidnap an ole lady of the club. They are getting braver and braver with their attacks.

I am tracking down all of the women that were taken, and have a list of all the members in the next surrounding three counties.

Clicking the message button, I shoot her a quick message, using my real image. Much to my surprise, I get a response instantly.

Little did I know that I would be rescuing her two months later. Saving her from the hell she was living in, a place where she was stuck and living a nightmare.

I sure as fuck didn't expect falling for her goofy ass.

That fucking smile that makes me turn into a pussy.

I wouldn't change one fucking thing about Alisha.

This is our story. Fucking enjoy it, or if you don't, fuck off.

Chapter One

Alisha

My phone starts ringing with a Facetime call, so I run across the room to grab it before my father can hear it. I just heard him outside my door a minute earlier, but I don't think he has left yet. My heart is pounding out of my chest at the thought of what he would do if he caught a man calling me.

I click the green button and climb into bed facing the door in case my father comes in. This way I can hide the phone before he can see. I stole the Wi-Fi password from the bottom of the router, and my father doesn't know I use it.

My friend gave me her iPhone she doesn't use anymore.

"Baby, what's the matter?" Jordan asks and I stare at the screen. I forgot I answered the call while I was still looking at the door.

"Nothing is wrong." I smile into the phone. Jordan is sitting at a desk surrounded by three huge computers.

"You sure? You looked scared for a second there," he asks again, his narrowed eyes demanding me to tell him what's wrong.

I can't do that.

It's not that simple. The life I am living isn't a normal one.

I met Jordan when I joined a dating site because I was lonely and needed someone to talk to. My friend left for college and left me in this hole in the wall community outside of Raleigh, Texas.

I am living in a trailer with my mom and dad. I don't want to be here. I am stuck; literally. I have no car and no way to get one, because the closest jobs are an hour away. The little community I am living in is for the people who want to live out their drug days and run from the cops. It's extremely dangerous. I quit going to school when I was fifteen; I am twenty-one years old now.

My mom and dad are always on drugs. My dad is fucked up in the head and abusive. The house I am living in is rat-infested, run down, and holes litter the ground so large you can stick your hand through them and touch the ground.

Jordan is a reprieve from the life I am living. The only haven I have is my room and Jordan. With him I can pretend my life isn't complete shit.

"Baby?" he asks again. I drifted off again. I look down at the phone and can see he's concerned. In the past two months, we have become close. He has offered to take me out, but I keep on refusing.

I don't want him to see the life I am living.

Jordan is so funny. He can make the worst day better with his cheesy jokes. Don't forget, he's absolutely gorgeous on top of having that bad boy look, complete with the tattoos. Protective. When I had a black eye and said I ran into the corner of the cabinet, he freaked out. He was pissed. Nobody has ever worried about me like that before.

The thing is, I never ran into a cabinet. My dad punched me in the face because I knocked over his drink. I walk on eggshells constantly, because anything can set him off.

"Why is this door locked?" my dad yells from outside of my room. My eyes widen in fear and I look at Techy. He's furious. "Jordan, I will call you back." I click end and hide my phone in the hole beside my wall, sliding a picture on top to cover it.

I walk over to my door slowly, my hands sweating. When I unlock the door, my stomach hits the floor. My body is jittery from the nerves.

My bedroom door flies open and hits the wall, hard.

I take a step back away from him, push a strand of my hair behind my ear, and stare at my father.

He is six foot tall and is skin and bones. His face is sunken in and his hair is stringy. Drugs and a poor diet will do that to you. Constant hunger is something I have become accustomed to.

"I will not ask again, bitch," he says and brings me out of my thoughts. I stare at him in sadness. I never had a father who cared about me. It's sad that I have become used to this.

"I was changing," I lie and try to look innocent.

He sneers at me and looks around my room. "Bull fucking shit. What were you doing?"

That's when the picture that covers the hidden hole in the wall falls down and my phone slides out and lands on the bed.

"What the fuck is this, bitch?" he roars in my face and stomps past me. I know I won't be walking for a week after this.

He picks up my phone and I see it's going off, Jordan's picture popping up as he Facetimes me.

"Who the fuck is this?" He shows me the screen. I close my eyes. Yeah, I am doomed.

"WHO THE FUCK IS THIS?" he screams in my face, spit flying out of his mouth, hitting me.

"Nobody," I say in a soft, meek voice. I am scared. Beyond scared. The thought of the beating I am about to get is looming in front of me.

"Well, we will see, won't we?" My father chuckles evilly as he thrusts the phone in my hand. "Answer it."

I shake my head no. I can't let Jordan see me like this. My father's face darkens and I gulp. He punches me in the nose. I flinch in pain. Blood is dripping down my face.

"ANSWER IT!" he roars again and tears well in my eyes.

I tap the green circle and his face pops onto my screen. I mouth 'I am sorry' to him. A million different emotions cross his face at the sight of me. I feel ashamed.

"Well, I see why you are hiding the phone, bitch." My father clucks his tongue and fists my hair.

"Take your fucking hands off of her or the whole fucking Devil's Souls MC will take your ass out," Jordan threatens my dad in a voice I haven't ever heard him use before. I look at him and he mouths 'I am coming for you.'

My dad throws the phone against the wall. It shatters into a million pieces.

"You just signed your death warrant, bitch," my dad screams in a high-pitch voice. He pulls his hand back and connects with my face. Then does it again and again. When I fall to the floor, he kicks me in the stomach. I curl into a ball as he steps on my hands, kicks my stomach anywhere he can get that will cause harm.

I black out and hold on to the hope that Jordan is coming for me. I can't live this life anymore.

Techy

"FUCKK!" I yell at the top of my lungs at the sight of Alisha with blood running down her face and a man fisting her hair in his hands hard. Her eyes filled with tears, lost, sad, and utterly alone.

Not anymore.

I run up the stairs of the basement where my office is and up into the clubhouse. I spot Butch, Vin, and Trey sitting at the bar shooting the shit. They look at my expression and stand up immediately.

"What is it, Techy?" Vin asks.

"I met this fucking girl online on a dating site when I was tracking down the fucking gang members. I couldn't get her fucking out of my mind. I messaged her two months ago, and we have been video chatting since. Someone was banging on her door right before she disconnected. I called back a minute later. She picked up with blood pouring down her face and a man's hand in her hair," I explain quickly, not even caring they know I met her online.

"Fuck, man," Butch says. I see him walking toward the door, ready to ride with me.

"She yours?" Trey asks and I look over at him. I nod and he nods back. He walks outside and Vin follows suit. Butch follows behind him and I run out, my gun in my holster, then climb on my Harley and floor it out of the parking lot.

The only thing between Alisha and me is the open highway.

No fucking woman should be hurt like that, especially her.

He is going to fucking pay with his life.

Alisha

I groan as I reach for a blanket that is hanging off my bed, drag it across the floor and under my head. I shiver and wince at the pain in my stomach. The tears running down my face feel like scalding hot water.

He has never beaten me this badly before. I knew it would be bad, but this is something else altogether. My body feels like one huge bruise. I know I won't be able to get up, so I decide to go to sleep here.

My mom is in the house; I've seen her look into my bedroom as he was kicking me, but all she did was turn around, as if this was something she sees every single day of her life. He hits her, too, but not like he does me.

I lie here all alone on my floor, crying, in pain, miserable, and I wish my life would end. I don't want to be in a world like this. I have a small bit of hope, and that is Jordan. He gave me something to look forward to, which is that maybe the rest of the world isn't as bad as my life.

There are good people in this world.

I just never met anyone good apart from him and my best friend.

I've been lying on the hard ground for thirty minutes when I hear the motorcycles. My heart stops in disbelief. *Has he come for me? He said he would.* I sob into my blanket. I could be free. The motorcycles get closer and closer until I know they are parked outside of my house. The broken-down trailer feels like it's shaking from the power of the motorcycles vibrating through the walls.

The trailer silences. The TV is turned off and all I can hear is the sound of my breathing until footsteps sound on our ratty porch and a couple of men talk. I strain to hear what they are saying. When I hear someone else speak, I recognize the voice.
Jordan.
He came for me.
I plant my hand on the ground and push myself over onto my stomach then lift with all of my might until I am on my knees. I pant in pain loudly. It's excruciating. I grab the edge of my bed and push myself up the rest of the wall, my body shaking from the exertion.

When I am standing, I bend in half, clutching at my stomach, and walk slowly to my bedroom door. I pull it open, my body screaming at me.

I hear a loud noise and my mom screaming. They must have kicked in the door. I hold on to the wall with one hand while the other grips my stomach. I clench my jaw at the pain and close my eyes to hold back the tears.

"Alisha!" Jordan calls and I spur forward, entering the kitchen, which is connected to the living room. I look up and see Jordan standing there with three other huge men. Techy is just as big. My knees start to give out and I grab the corner of the wall to hold myself up.

"Where is she?" Jordan roars at my dad. My dad starts apologizing. Jordan pinches the bridge of his nose and walks over to my dad, throws his fist back, and punches him right in the face. My dad falls back to the floor, out cold. I stare in disbelief at how he can knock someone out with one punch.

I just want to be held right now; and I want that to be Jordan. I want to be as far away from this place as possible.

"Jordan," I say softly

His eyes connect with mine and I see fury once he looks me over. I feel ashamed. Jordan runs over. He stops when he is a hairbreadth away from me and touches my face. I wince at the smallest of touches then let go of the wall and wrap my arms around his waist.

I let out a deep breath as I feel his warmth, the strength of his chest, close my eyes, and sink farther into his body, letting him hold me. I don't care about the pain. All I know in this moment is I feel like I belong somewhere for the first time in my life and that everything will be okay.

"Baby, I am so fucking sorry," he whispers. I shake my head no. "You didn't know, Jordan," I whisper back.

"I am taking you away from here. You will never see this fucking place again," he says vehemently.

"Let's go," I whisper and look up at him as Jordan stares into my eyes. "Nothing will harm you again." I close my eyes at the feelings running through me. I feel protected, safe.

"Okay," is all I can manage to get out before I black out from exhaustion, the pain, and everything that has happened today. I feel him catch me; and then there's darkness.

Techy

I catch Alisha as she passes out and pick her up bridal style then turn around and look at my brothers. They look at the girl in my arms, and it's fucking heartbreaking how messed up she looks. She is five foot nothing and one hundred and twenty pounds at a push. Even through the cuts and bruises you can see how beautiful she is.

"Man, she's fucked up," Vinny says. I set her down on the couch, turn to her father, who is now waking up from when I knocked him out. I kick him in the side and he startles awake.

I knew the moment I got a good fucking look at the man sitting here in this living room, these were her parents. She has her dad's fucking eyes and hair color. Her stature is just like her mother's. Her mother is so strung out, she is fucking just staring into space, with drool running down her chin.

I pull my gun out of my pocket and twist the silencer onto the tip. "Vin, cover her ears." Her dad wakes up and stares at me in disbelief as I click the silencer into place. He starts shaking his head no. I bend down until I am eye-level with him.

"Please," he whispers and his putrid breath hits my face.

"Death is too easy for you, but I don't have time to torture you, waiting for you to beg me to kill you. Enjoy hell," I say lastly and stand up. I grab a pillow and place it between his head and the gun so the blood doesn't splatter on me. He cries, begs, pleads. I click the safety off and pull the trigger. He slumps against the ground. Then I stare at her mother. She is still staring into space. Fucking pathetic.

Vinny lets go of Alisha's ears, and I hand my gun to Butch, the sergeant at arms. He nods and stuffs it in his pocket. He will get rid of it and make sure it will never be found. I walk over to Alisha and pick her up off the ground.

Then I carry her from this fucking hell.

No looking back. I climb on my bike and Trey takes her from my arms and turns her around until she is front to front with me. He lifts her legs and sets them on top of my legs. I tuck my leather jacket around her and wrap my arm around her back, holding her to my chest. Fuck, she's fucking tiny.

"Call Myra and have her meet me at my house." Trey nods and opens his phone. I look down at the girl in my arms out cold. Then I start the motorcycle, tighten my grip on her, and speed out of this fucking place.

acknowledgements

To all my fans! I am astonished at the amount of support I have gotten since I revealed I was publishing this book. Your excitement, made everything worth it and million times more. Without you guys I wouldn't be a author. <3

To my review team members that loved my books since day one. You kept encouraging me to continue and I thank you for that.

Brooke Miller, my best friend. I want to thank you for being such an amazing friend! <3

Emily, for helping me with my million a one questions.

The Hype PR for handing my cover reveal and release.

To everyone that promotes my work everything you do is a huge help and means the world to me.

To everyone that has helped me along this journey. Without you I wouldn't be here today.

Thank you.

about the author

LeAnn Asher's is a blogger turned author who released her debut novel early 2016 and can't wait to see where this new adventure takes her. LeAnn writes about strong-minded females and strong protective males who love their women unconditionally.

Facebook Page: www.facebook.com/Leannashers
Twitter: @LeannAshers
Email: Authorleannasher@gmail.com

More from LeAnn Ashers

Forever Series

Protecting His Forever
Loving His Forever

Devil Souls MC Series

Torch
Techy
Butcher
Liam

Grim Sinners MC Series

Lane
Wilder

Printed in Great Britain
by Amazon